Pine Valley Series : Book Two

MOTHERS

OF

PINE WAY

CORRINE ARDOIN

Black Rose Writing | Texas

First printing

This is a work of fiction. Names, characters, businesses, places, events, and incidents are either the products of the author's imagination or used in a fictitious manner. Any resemblance to actual persons, living or dead, or actual events is purely coincidental.

ISBN: 978-1-68433-683-8
PUBLISHED BY BLACK ROSE WRITING
www.blackrosewriting.com

Printed in the United States of America
Suggested Retail Price (SRP) $18.95

Mothers of Pine Way is printed in Garamond

*As a planet-friendly publisher, Black Rose Writing does its best to eliminate unnecessary waste to reduce paper usage and energy costs, while never compromising the reading experience. As a result, the final word count vs. page count may not meet common expectations.

This book is dedicated to my mother...
who told me the stories I needed to hear,
...and to the ancestors.

MOTHERS

OF

PINE WAY

PROLOGUE

Candelaria sat at the front of the church, a grieving daughter at her mother's funeral Mass. Wearing a black dress she wore to her husband's funeral, a gold chain necklace from the thrift store its only adornment, she sighed and waited. Her tired, old, black shoes squeezed her feet. The veil itched her scalp. Lips barely moving, she distracted herself, quietly rehearsing a poem she planned to recite. When the time came to do so, Father Sanchez signaled her to approach the lectern. Seeing him waiting for her, sobs rose in her throat. She tried to stand, but felt herself begin to shake. The priest hurried to her side, asking if she would be okay. Composing herself, she nodded. One foot stepped before the other until she stood behind the lectern and began.

"This is a poem I wrote for my mother, to honor her, and to tell her that I love her."

Her mind went blank. Fortunately, she noticed the piece of paper before her. It was her poem. Gathering her strength, she raised her head, recognizing the sad, expectant faces looking her way. Reciting from memory, she said, "To Mother." Floating on the words, she continued, "Sweet mother, how you flew on

Grace's wings! You taught me everything! Now, you are gone. The lifting boughs have granted your way home on autumn winds. I learned to live my life by you, to teach my heart to fly like you. Like a dove? No. Like the sparrow. You asked for so little, yet gave so much...in your song that rose from high: your laughter...in your dance that swelled the heights: your very breath. This is for you, dear one, my lovely mother, my beautiful, sweet sparrow. I look for you every evening upon the wind!"

CHAPTER ONE

Turning toward the ruined house in flames, Ev brought to mind one special day. Boughs of fir and pine, rain glistening upon their branches, appeared within her view. An old house in disrepair and children playing upon the lawn with their dog, she recalled with joy, and smiled. Hopes and dreams stirred within her heart. They were as fresh as the rain in her memories. Returning to the present, and the great loss taking place, her strength wavered. She could not find the will to leave.

They waited for her, looking one to another, knowing how difficult it must be for their aging friend. Though they gave her time in silence, the sun would not. It rose behind the mountains to the east, climbing its high arc across the sky, to eventually reach beyond the gathering clouds and begin lowering behind the mountains in the west. They needed to go before stars appeared in the autumn sky. All the daylight hours were needed to make the first day's journey toward their destination.

"Come on, Ev." Ev's young friend lightly pulled on her arm, urging her to come with them. Becoming impatient and irritated with the old woman, she tugged again. "It's time to go."

Defeated and unable to look anymore, Ev walked away.

3

• • •

Pioneers, they once were called, the older residents of Pine Way by the younger ones in Edenville. Ev's mother told her stories about the real pioneers. They traveled in long wagon trains, like a narrow stream. Her mother, Estefana Garcia, was among them, a young girl with a dream. "Goin' out West," she said.

Ev remembered her mother telling the story. They were always talking and planning, preparing for months. Their restlessness spread like a prairie fire of excitement, the dream ignited. But, the story turned tragic. Her mother's eyes grew big and stared upward toward the sky as she shared the experience with her daughter.

"They came on horseback, the men, with torches burning. We heard the thundering of hooves. The dust raised all around the settlers' cabins. They came in a sudden sweep of anger, flames alighting onto rugs and cushions as they flung their torches crashing through the window panes!"

Her mother said she heard someone scream. Later, sitting in the wagon while the families were departing, she realized the truth. It was she who screamed, for no one else in her family was left alive. Her brothers died from the fever and her parents were killed. At this part of the story, her eyes filled with tears, telling Ev, "I was alone and merely movin' on."

When Ev's mother told the story, Ev envisioned herself on the wagon train. She could almost feel the rocking and clunking kind of rolling along of the wagon's big wooden wheels. She saw the tall grass flowing in the wind. Her mother said the prairie was so flat you could see far, far away. Huge flocks of birds startled and took to wing in a flutter of yellows and golds. It was a grand adventure across a new land. Their dream kept them going, toward some distant place over the great mountains.

"Pine Way," Ev whispered softly to herself. "Pine Way."

She leaned over to get a pine branch from the ground to use as a walking stick. Tapping one end, she tested its sturdiness. Delighting in the memory her mother's story nurtured in her long ago, she pretended to be on the wagon train. When the real pioneers first saw the valley, her mother said, they paused to admire the forested view, more peaceful than they dreamed. Pine, fir, oak, and great maple trees drew them onward, gradually descending the last mountain ridge. The sweet scent in the air smelled fresh and calmed their restless spirits. Climbing down off their wagons, others who arrived the year before, rushed to greet them. The reality of their long trek came to Ev's mother especially, because her parents, her brothers, her entire family lay buried far away. She had no family.

Maria Evangelica Theresa Garcia became Ev Mendoza when she married. Ev believed she knew something of what her mother's story revealed. Her house also burned down, her family's treasures and belongings destroyed. She embarked upon a long trek, ignorant of their destination. The small group of people she agreed to join, "Chicanos," they called themselves, were supposedly marching to the state capital on behalf of all her people, not Mexican, though not American, either, somehow. She failed to understand. Marching, protesting, activism? You work hard, save your money, pray for a decent job, take care of your family! What else is there? Reaching to pick up another pine branch she spotted along the way, she used it for a walking stick instead, laying the other aside.

The people with whom she walked had a faster pace, youngsters to her. They kept stopping to wait. She wore an old-fashioned housedress, reaching well below her knees, and braided her long, gray hair. To protect against the cold, she wore a bulky, drab brown sweater, buttoned up to her chin, with huge cuffs on the sleeves. Tired already, she kept going, regardless, even as they reached the edge of town. She could have encouraged them to go on without her. Something compelled her to keep going, so she remained quiet.

They asked her daughter, Candelaria Hart, who lost her husband years ago. She declined going on the march but urged Ev to participate. Walking out of town, onto the highway, Ev wondered how far they would walk that day. Asking her companions, they said miles. So, she said a prayer. Not long after dark, they finally reached their night's encampment, where supporters met them. Everyone was busy preparing for the next day's walking.

Seeing Ev so tired and drawn, some grew concerned. Helping her into the house, a woman who lived there gave her a bed, so she could rest for the next day. Others talking amongst themselves agreed it was best she stayed behind, while someone hastily tossed the pine branch into the weeds by the door.

Ev vaguely heard gasps of astonishment about her house burning down that morning. Why did she leave? Who allowed her to come? She could hear them bickering.

Her young friend surreptitiously glanced toward her. From where the young woman stood in the dimly lit kitchen, arms folded in front of her, she looked on as someone covered Ev with a blanket and gave her water to drink. Ev refused food, turning her head away when they put a spoon to her mouth. Someone carefully dabbed Ev's face with a damp cloth, her scattered whiskers springing back when her wrinkled chin was wiped.

Their voices grew distant as Ev drifted to sleep. Among the last things she heard was the screen door thump shut and her young friend striking up a match to light a cigarette.

Exasperated, another woman scolded the girl. "Tsk! Why don't you quit that dirty habit?!"

The young friend, coughing, replied impatiently, "I know! I know!"

A man sang "La Paloma" outdoors, accompanied by a softly played guitar. Another song followed, a song of empowerment, uniting them toward their cause. Hopeful, distant voices joined in, singing to lift their spirits, to keep them going, and to strengthen their resolve.

That night, Ev dreamed her house was new again. Walking through the front doorway, everything looked like when she was young, her husband so handsome and her children only babies. By morning, she had grown weaker, her breath faint and her body still. While not asleep, her eyes were closed, busy watching a river flowing past, a river of her life and accomplishments, now behind her. Up she went to the ceiling, and thought it funny, wondering why, until her parents came to her as though from a dream. When she reached for them, she saw her arms, young and smooth. Her mother and father were happy, both of them so beautiful.

"Come on, Ev." They put their arms around her waist and turned to walk across a green field. "Let's go home."

She told them, "No. Let me see my daughter one last time." They released her. Strangely, she was back on the bed, knowing she still had time.

CHAPTER TWO

Candelaria received word that her mother became gravely ill during the night after marching with the migrant farmworkers. Most of the older resident laborers of Edenville refrained from participating. They said it was foolish to risk losing their jobs. A woman told her over the phone that one of the marchers was a doctor. He said her mother was old. It was simply her time. Candelaria worried once she hung up the phone. Allowing her mother to join in the march was a fatal mistake. Sobbing for the nearing loss of her mother and the loss of her childhood home, the guilt trying to creep in had no room to stay. When she heard a car pull up outside, she stuffed her wet handkerchief into her apron pocket and left.

Traveling along the highway, she noticed her son, Jim, behaving disinterested. She nudged his arm, inquiring, "So?" She was trying to bring him back, her son who lived a life of secrets of which she was not a part, a life of which she knew he never dreamed, only what turned out to be his life.

"So...what?!" He glanced quickly at her, bothered and anxious, then back at the road, trying not to let show what he needed to tell her. He planned to move to the city, divorce his wife, and start fresh. Sensing it was a bad time to tell her, he relaxed.

After a while, they arrived at the house where marchers were assembling. A few were beginning to depart, carrying picket signs and banners. Several wore brown berets and acted like soldiers.

Jim disliked them. Irritated, he mumbled to himself, "Why do they have to act like that?" They came to Edenville during the summer, trying to rouse the pickers, so he frowned their way. "Why did they have to come here and make trouble?" He decided to stay in the car away from the commotion, wishing he could disappear. An image came to mind of someone he loved, the way she looked the last time they were together. He preferred this image to the scene taking place beyond his car.

Candelaria, amazed at how far her mother walked, absentmindedly untied her apron while looking at the other people. She tossed it onto the front seat and shut the car door. Looking at her son, she saw him leaning back in the seat, a thumbnail between his teeth, his eyes gazing far away. Sighing heavily, she walked away from the car, unable to do anything about him.

Not recognizing any of the people leaving to continue the march, she wondered where they lived. She thought for a moment that she would rather head back to the car and tell her son, "Let's get out of here!" They could put her mother in the back seat and leave before anyone noticed. She admonished herself. "Why did I think my mother would like this?! What was I thinking?!"

Mechanically, she willed herself to approach the house. A man with a megaphone was giving a pep talk for the day, directing everyone. She opened the screen door and stepped inside the small dwelling, barely feeling a part of her own body, having become more like a pair of eyes floating in mid-air. Unnoticed by her were the lingering smells of breakfast cooked earlier. The smoky smell of burnt bacon and rich odors from greasy fried eggs and potatoes cooked in bacon fat, yet filled the air. She felt nothing as someone escorted her to a bedroom, barely hearing one woman's questions, then apologies. The light touch of another's hand upon her arm went ignored. But, once she entered the bedroom, something from within herself took hold and, in her next breath, the smells filling the entire house came to life. Though unseen, a mildewed shower curtain down the hall and a clogged toilet, blended with burnt toast and bitter, strong coffee. The few who stood near became an oppressive crowd.

Her mother lay upon a small bed, perhaps that of a child's, whose frayed and threadbare, flowered quilt now served to comfort an old woman. Her eyes were closed, her hands clasped upon her chest. For some reason, the only thing Candelaria registered in her sight was but a weathered little girl with white hair. Grief and revulsion suddenly struck her and it rose like a wave. Finally, she relented and began sobbing convulsively. Reaching for the bed, as everyone else left the room, she barely caught herself before her legs gave way and she flopped down beside her mother.

Ev remarked, "I'm not dead, yet."

Candelaria stiffened, snapping out of her shock. While seated on the bed, her arms wrapped tightly around herself, she gently rocked forward and back, mumbling something, unconsciously engaging in an old childhood habit. In minutes, she stopped.

Done with crying for now, she wiped her eyes and nose with the back of her hand.

So serious, she thought. She could almost laugh, telling herself, "You better not!" She looked out the bedroom window, spotting her son combing his hair and checking it in the rearview mirror. Out the bedroom doorway, across the kitchen, she beheld the marchers outside walking away. One girl dropped her end of a banner, and the wind caught it, while the other girl stood by, laughing at her. A dog wandered around the yard, scratching itself, before snatching up one of the lunch sacks left behind and dashing off with it between its teeth. Yet, oh! She could laugh hysterically at Life now. "Such fools we are," she thought aloud. "God knows it. And, now, you know it, too. Don't you, Mamá?"

The house was quiet. Outside, a light breeze stirred the leaves in the trees. Chickens complained in that way they have, squawking and whining. Candelaria kissed her mother's forehead, about to get up and leave the room, when her mother spoke again. Caressing her mother's forehead, tears came, but they were gentle and felt good, so she let them come.

"Laria."

"Yes, Mamá."

"The old house . . ."

"I know."

"The men did it. They threw the torches in!"

"No, Mamá. No." Candelaria corrected her mother while gently patting her hand. "That was your mother's house. That was before you were born."

The best Candelaria could do was try to calm her. "Shhh," she said. It was what her mother used to do for her, when she was a child, gently smooth her hair and say, "There, there." It worked.

"Okay." Her mother, like a little girl, agreed, though she needed to say more. Her heart was breaking. She cried, "I'm sorry, Laria! I should have...let...go away to college."

Candelaria covered her face with one hand and cried all the more. She, Candelaria, did nothing when her son was to go away to college and decided not to, because his father died. She sensed her mother needed to unburden herself, grasping for— But, no more words came, only a final breath, and Ev was gone. Candelaria put her hand to her face, crying out in her grief, then groaning and wailing, her shoulders shaking.

The few people in the house and out in the yard guessed what took place. The old woman died. The one who was hanging laundry on the clothesline stopped what she was doing and blessed herself with the sign of the cross, kissing her closed hand afterward. "Pobrecita," she said.

Jim entered the house. Looking in on his mother and grandmother, he wiped his hand over his face and around the back of his neck. Ready to do what needed to be done, he inquired, "So, are we gonna go now, or what?" He kept a bottle of liquor under his car seat and was drinking from it, waiting in the car to give his mother privacy. Judging by the stern look on his mother's face, he figured he did something wrong.

Candelaria was aware of her son's drinking, wondering who this bloodshot-and-glassy-eyed boy was, standing before her as though they were getting ready to leave for the grocery store. He shaved and was strong and was grown, but he never grew up, she believed. She could no longer stand to look at him. Her heart told her "no more."

She left her mother's side, brushing past him to look for someone in the house, to ask if she could use the phone. Having gone through this experience before, she wanted to get it done. Once she walked across the kitchen, a sudden daze came over her. She clutched the back of a chair to brace herself. Closing her eyes, she sensed something within her fall to the ground in defeat as the victor rose to claim her heart and soul. Fearless, she gathered her strength to face it.

CHAPTER THREE

The morning her grandmother's house burned down, Rosa Hart arrived when the volunteer fire department was leaving. She dreaded speaking with them.

The driver stopped and questioned her from his truck window, "Where'd Ev go? She was here with a bunch of people... They all just walked off down the road," sweeping his hand through the air. He tipped his oversized hard hat back with his fingers, explaining, "We need some information from her to put in our report."

Rosa looked away, not wanting to talk to him.

The captain of the volunteer fire department softened his tone. "Okay." His oversized breakfast suddenly churned in his gut. He needed to get going. Pushing his hard hat back again, he added, "Well, soon as you get a chance, bring her over to the station, all right?"

Rosa nodded her head quickly and continued down her grandmother's driveway, blurting out, "Station?!" Their town fire station was someone's garage. The house it went with was long gone. Momentarily disgusted, she further scoffed, "Probably burned down!"

When she reached the clearing where a house once stood, she parked the car and got out, staring at the sodden, blackened heap before her. The sour smell of burned and wet wood, the puddles and mud that met her eyes, revolted her. It was like a greasy wet barbecue pit the size of a swimming pool. Stepping closer, her white sweater slipped from her shoulders and fell to the dirt.

"This was Grandma's house." She placed one hand to the side of her face while the other rested on her hip.

A glimpse of color amidst the black and gray drew her closer. She realized there may be valuables buried in the rubble, something worth saving. Although, she was not dressed for the task. She got ready to go to work at the beauty parlor, first rushing over to see the fire. Her clothes, her shoes, her— She spotted her sweater in the dirt. Moving quickly, as though leaping to save a child before it was hit by a car, she grabbed up her sweater and instantly began crying. Her father died years ago, leaving no one to whom she could turn, to take care of things, take care of her and her mother. Her brother, Jim Hart, was sadly unreliable and unpredictable. Now this! Resigning herself, she wiped her tears away, set the sweater on the car hood, and surveyed the scene.

The old house lacked a foundation, so it was too hazardous to step onto the mess of jumbled boards. Glancing over the pile of debris, she spotted someone on the other side of it, a man wearing blue denim pants and a white t-shirt. He was bent down, looking around, and picking through the blackened lumber. Angry, she felt a sudden surge of strength, like she could do anything, and shouted to him, "Hey! You there!" For a moment, she waited for him to respond, but the man must not have heard, she assumed. Turning away to begin her search, she located an old, wooden garden stake and pulled it out of the ground. Poking and digging around the edges of the pile, she soon forgot about the man, until he stood next to her. Almost falling over in fright, she yelled, "Forty! What are you doing here?!" She recognized Fortuitous Sumner, a man her grandmother said always acted like a private investigator.

Barely audible, he said, "Uh, hello, Rosa." He was looking up and down and away, anywhere except directly at her. "Just thought I'd keep an eye on the place. You never know who might come by and make mischief."

Standing up, Rosa's mouth opened in shocking disbelief. Forty had one hand under his shirt, sliding over his belly, while his other hand was flattening his greased hair. It popped up again. He straightened himself to stand proudly as though he was going to say the pledge of allegiance.

Forty recalled something he read about women in the summer issue of *Detective's Digest*. It said they needed a man to be the strong one, someone to whom they could turn. The thought inspired him. He felt courageous and proud to play such a role.

Nevertheless, his playacting annoyed Rosa. She had no time or patience for him, so she walked away to continue rummaging through the heap.

Fortuitous, not sure what else to do, except take care of her, followed behind. Soon, he resumed digging around again. It was not long before he heard Rosa talking. He saw something in her hand and asked, "Is it valuable?"

Even though Forty bothered her, Rosa patiently replied, "No, just a keepsake. I'm surprised to find it. It was on a shelf at this end of the house. I forgot all about it." She rubbed it, trying to remove the blackened grime. It was a portrait of her mother as a young girl in pigtails, smiling big and showing her missing teeth. A small silver frame held the old sepia print behind glass.

Nevertheless, Rosa grew increasingly ill-at-ease. Forty moved closer, looking over her shoulder, his hot and straining breath blowing at the back of her head. She stood up and backed away from him. He promptly stood at attention by her side. Exasperated, she decided to leave for the beauty parlor, promising herself she would return after work. Forty went back to rooting around through the debris.

Lingering next to her car, Rosa gazed upon her surroundings. Clouds almost covered the sky. Birds raucously sang in the tall elm trees lining the road. She remembered playing here as a child. Her family, her mother and father, and her brother lived here before they moved into the house where Jim and his wife now lived. Her father ran the blacksmith shop and livery stable. Her mother, Candelaria Hart, worked in the orchards as a farm laborer, despite her father's protests. Unlike him, her mother was Mexican, and her mother's parents, going all the way back to Mexico, Rosa assumed. It was something she rarely pondered. Her life growing up in Pine Way, her awareness, was that of a child among many children playing on their street. Her grandmother babysat her and her brother often, but never spoke of the old, old days, except for a story she used to tell, how her great-grandmother, Estefana Garcia, came to the valley. Rosa faintly remembered her grandfather, who was older than her grandmother, but he died a long time ago.

Her scattered thoughts flowed along, a brief sense of the past and her childhood days. She remembered family gatherings held at this house. She remembered playing with their dog on the lawn that, years ago, dried and withered away to dust, and she remembered playing tag with her cousins. The dog... What was its name? Curly? She barely remembered the nondescript mutt, a brown and gray, tangle-haired pooch her brother had been given...by whom? Her scattered memories traced their way from days of laughter she unknowingly mourned. Her life changed so fast! Now, those days were gone. What a waste, she thought. The great loss left her aggrieved and tired, wanting to drive away and never return.

Forty shouted, "I found something! I found something!"

He hastened toward her holding a shiny medallion on a ribbon. Rosa instantly recognized her brother's football medal he received during his graduation. Her grandmother kept it on a shelf in her room with some other memorabilia from his high school football career.

"Thank you, Forty," she told him as he stood near her, beaming. "I think I'm gonna leave now. I'll come back another time to look some more." She hurriedly got in her car, starting it up without delay. Absentmindedly, she leaned over and popped open the glove box, stuffing their meager findings inside, then closing it shut as she left for work.

Forty deduced she was overcome with emotion by what he found. He silently congratulated himself for a job well done.

He was off work that day. Earlier, he spotted the smoke from his porch, before he drove his wife, Sylvia, to the beauty parlor for a haircut, of which he disapproved. She stepped off the porch in a sky-blue, drop-waisted dress with pale blue and emerald green trim. She wore her hat and gloves, too, he noticed. She sat on the passenger side of the convertible, having never learned how to drive, while he scooped up his keys from the porch railing. Sitting behind the wheel of the car, he believed he must appear so manly to his wife, taking charge of things. She was so pretty and walked with such poise, ever so gracefully, he thought. Forty adored his wife and worked hard to provide for her.

He was off in a cloud of dust, reminding himself to check on the smoke, taking into account that his neighbor, Ev Mendoza, often burned piles of leaves. On their way into town, bumping onto the paved section of the street and bouncing a little, they passed the fire truck racing toward Pine Way. Forty stopped to watch them drive past. Going at least twenty miles per hour, when they met the dirt section of road, the truck dropped suddenly. One of the firemen fell off the back. He ran to jump on the truck when they stopped to wait for him. Forty wanted more than anything to turn his car around and follow them, but he had to take Sylvia into town first.

He dropped her off at Snip it in the Bud, the beauty parlor in the shopping center, where no one knew her. She said they were friendlier and charged less. Her thriftiness pleased him. Watching her walk into the beauty parlor, he said goodbye to her long, beautiful hair. Although, in a hurry and thinking he might be needed by the firemen, he put his car in reverse and spun around, charging across the parking lot, forcing other drivers to slam on their brakes. Speeding by their staring, gaping faces, Forty affirmed his importance to the community. He mentally reminded himself to order a stick-on, revolving police light he saw advertised in a recent issue of *Detective's Digest*. He thrilled at the idea he could put it on top of his car at these times, never mind he owned a convertible. Once he hit the dirt section of the street which led to the old town of Pine Way, he said aloud, briskly and with confidence, "Chester Ferguson, on the way!"

He decided to park at home and walk toward Ev's house, alert to anything out of the ordinary. The possibility that it was an accident never occurred to someone like Forty Sumner. He kept an eye on the place whenever he saw Ev Mendoza's housekeeper drive by his house. He missed seeing her car that day. All too suspicious to him, the young woman appearing in their neighborhood only a few months ago.

He reached Ev's house when the volunteer fire department finished extinguishing the fire. Approaching them, as though he were a county official, or the man, himself, in charge and checking in on them, he walked confidently, flipping and swinging his jingling keys around his fingers. He caught them giving each other a knowing glance and issuing a slight chuckle amongst themselves, shaking their heads.

He disregarded it, reminding himself, "No one likes the detective showing up at the scene of the crime. That's because he's distrustful of everyone and always solves the case in the end." Eyes narrowed, he said to himself, "Everyone's a suspect to Chester Ferguson!"

While they collected the blackened and wet hose, Forty studied the captain's movements. The man walked purposefully, making sure the fire was completely out, Forty assumed. Eager to get to work, he impatiently shot darting glances from one end of the burn to the other, looking for clues. The captain and his crew loaded the truck and began driving away. A second, pale green fire truck, slowly followed behind them, lumbering past Forty, its handful of crew members staring blankly at him. One man piqued Forty's interest. Experiencing a fleeting sense that he had seen the young man before, he was unable to remember, so disregarded it. Later, he would recall.

CHAPTER FOUR

At her daughter's house, Ev Mendoza lay in repose on an old army cot Jim found beneath the little shack. People arrived, some bearing pans and dishes of food, some with a story to share, many of them weeping and forlorn. Occasionally, they smiled or quietly laughed in remembrance of something Ev had said or had done.

"One time," a man said, "she pulled a prank on me and Freddie and Joseph." The man was seated on a folding chair and had one hand on Ev's shoulder. His smile grew wider and his eyes twinkled like a little boy's. "We used to help as altar boys during Mass and, when Father wasn't looking, we'd sneak some wine." He put his drawn fingers to his lips. "Or, peek in the cabinets." His fingers opened imaginary cupboards. "One time, one of us...I think it was Freddie. He was putting on Father's robe, with the hat and everything!" By this time, the storyteller was giggling. He unknowingly patted and grabbed Ev's shoulder in his enthusiasm while he swung his other arm to better express himself. "Oh, boy, then Ev walked in and caught us!" He laughed. "She cleaned the church for years. She said Father always carried around a notepad, telling us he was keeping a list of all our sins to give to the Devil. She said Father would give him our names and addresses, too, so he could come after us! We knew about that notepad!"

His hand patted the shoulder and his voice lowered. "Boy! We had to get that notepad away from Father before he gave it to the Devil! So, we watched him, each of us taking turns to see when he set it down." The man was unable to keep still until his eyes cast downward at Ev's face. Quickly, he drew his hand away, realizing he was touching Ev Mendoza and she was dead.

A mist drew over his eyes. In a hushed voice, he continued speaking. "Father called us into his office one morning after Stations of the Cross and told us, 'All right, you three! Out with it!' Boy, and he meant business, too!" The man took off his hat and held it by the brim down between his legs, watching as he turned it around and around. "I know now, he already knew what was going on. *Man!* That guy knows *everything!* We told him and he turned it into a lesson." His lower lip quivered as tears rolled down. "I'll never forget that." He rubbed his eyes and sniffed, his hat dropping to the floor. Pretending it was accidental, he bent over to retrieve it, so he could grieve unnoticed.

Candelaria anxiously busied herself in the kitchen setting a stack of paper plates alongside the food. She listened to the story, wishing everyone would leave so she could be alone. She remembered her mother without their help. Out came the memories as though from a movie that was her life. Her mother used to play like Betty Boop, singing and dancing, her father clapping his hands and stomping one foot to the beat, and whistling at her. What happened to the singing? She, herself, used to dance before her husband died, before life became so serious.

Her mother often tried to get her to smile. Candelaria recalled one instance in particular. They were having their morning coffee at the kitchen table. The bags and dark circles under her eyes were prominent that day.

"Laria . . ."

She knew her mother's way to first see if you were paying attention before she repeated herself.

"Laria . . ."

Usually, Candelaria half-heartedly played along. "Yes, Mamá."

Pleased, her mother delightfully continued, "Remember that time I was on television?"

"Yes, I remember."

Ev was a passerby in the background, making faces and dancing funny while a news story was being filmed.

"How did that dance go?"

Candelaria knew her mother was trying to get her to laugh. At first, she played along. After her husband died, she instead answered, "Oh, Mamá! Not now! I don't want to play your games!"

Candelaria felt badly. She asked herself, "What was so hard about making an old woman happy? That little old lady never hurt anybody."

Not able to take it anymore, she escaped out the front door, the screen gradually closing behind her. But, her reprieve from grief was short-lived. A car approached on the road, splashing in puddles left by the rain that fell earlier in the day. It was her son's light-blue-gray Ford Fairlane. "Four p.m.," she told him. The funeral home people were due to arrive at four o'clock. She wanted him there to help. Her daughter had to go to work. They needed the money more than ever now. Her eyebrows pinched together in anger and disappointment. She saw him driving in that certain way he had when he was drinking. He would go a little too fast and brake a little too sudden. She returned inside the house, unable to face him.

The funeral home people arrived. The little houses their eyes first beheld were all the same, unpainted, rustic, three-room cabins on stilts built as temporary housing for the migrant farmworkers. The people who lived in these two rows of seven or eight shanties, became permanent residents years ago. Fruit pickers and farm laborers, a tractor driver, a school teacher, a mechanic, and a gas station attendant, a motley sort, soon stepped out onto their porches, some with babies in arms. Wide-eyed and curious children peeked through windows and railings to see the big, shiny black hearse parked at Candelaria's.

One small boy, holding a tortilla with potato and meat rolled in it, made a show of tiptoeing toward the big car, looking back at his audience, grinning impishly. A sudden reprimand from his mother sent him scrambling back to hide behind her legs. Her aproned dress was blowing in the breeze. Smells from her kitchen, of hamburger meat and potatoes fried in a greasy pan, wafted in the air. She had one hand on her child to keep him behind her and one hand to frame the side of her woeful-looking face.

The people watching were in awe, in reverence, and in fear, lest the spirit of the dead visit them in the night. Their homes were up high, with plenty of storage space underneath used fully by everyone. Car parts, old furniture, and appliances were prominent. The men from the funeral home glanced around briefly, standing like grim specters in their gray suits, arms dangling with nothing for them to do, except wait for someone to meet them by the steps.

Candelaria's son brought with him a large box he carried around to the back of the house. She caught a glimpse, then went into the bathroom, not wanting to see what was coming. Again, she wished she could be left alone. Her father and mother, her siblings when they were little, everyone visited upon her. She struggled to cope with the relentless upwelling. Although, something else began erupting through the years of silence since her husband's death. She knew it was coming. She felt it right after her mother died.

Jim greeted the men. He shook their hands, freeing them from the watchful neighbors, one drying her hands on a towel, looking concerned. The men opened up the back of the hearse. Jim led them into the house, the soles of their nice black shoes scuffing the grit on each step. He helped them carry the unlined box his grandmother was in and slide it into the back of the vehicle.

One woman began crying. Her husband put his arm around her. She turned toward him to hide from the awful sight and to bury her grief in his embrace.

Jim shook each man's hand again, nodding his head while he did so, to say goodbye and thank you. Sitting in the front seat of the hearse, they each wiped their shoes with a small white cloth before drawing their feet into the car and slowly driving away. Inside the house, he kindly asked everyone to leave. On their way out, they each carried a plateful of food heaped high, slices of cake, and cups of punch. The flooring strained and creaked beneath shuffling feet. They were talking amongst themselves, reminding Jim to tell his mother to call on them for anything she might need. Someone told Jim he looked real nice. They were proud of him for taking care of things since his father died. Others nodded in agreement or lightly patted him on the back.

They drove away or walked to their own little houses. Jim folded up the cot, his wavy, dark brown hair falling down over his face. He pushed it back again and continued tidying, folding the chairs, tucking them neatly under the house with the cot.

He guessed his mother was in the bathroom, hoping to avoid her. Earlier in the day, he nearly emptied a bottle of Jack Daniel's he was trying to hide from his wife. After eating some of the food, he made up a couple of plates to take home, excitedly grabbing some spareribs he knew his dogs would love. Out the door, closing it behind, he was off to his own house, near where his grandmother's once stood. He felt nothing but hunger, neither love nor hate nor even a pretend indifference. In truth, he was numb, and planned to stay that way until it was over.

Candelaria breathed a sigh of relief. She was finally alone. By some mysterious signal, she quickly rose to her feet and cast off the shadowy cloak she unconsciously hid beneath since her husband's death. It was the darkness of her mourning time within which she could no longer bear to hide. Eyes wide and wild, she dug through an old shoebox on an apple crate by the bathroom sink and drew out a pair of scissors. Hesitantly, at first, then furiously, she gained momentum, grabbing chunks of her long hair with one hand and cutting them off with the scissors in her other hand. It was almost pre-planned or calculated, an act that stood poised and ready for this moment, suddenly released from the gate and given permission to run at last. She was done mourning her husband and was now like a woman gripping the bars of her cell where she squatted, giving birth to what was emerging.

Grabbing and hacking, she pulled and cut the long, thick clumps of dark brown hair. They fell into the sink, onto her shoulders, and down to the floor. A desperate cry, almost like a frantic panting raced out of her heart and soul, hacking away and dismembering the dead body of her former self, the Mexican woman who now knew *she* was Chicano. She, Candelaria Mendoza, not really Mexican, though not really American, either. At least not yet, for she knew this truth was what the fight was about at its core: to become fully accepted, with a place in the whole of all people and all things and all places American.

When she was done, panting and heaving and shaking violently, she came to at the sight of her sacrificial rite, her cherished hair strewn and piled everywhere, breathlessly speaking, "Oh, my God! Oh, my God!" She hurriedly scooped it up, stuffing it into a paper sack by the sink, praying to that which gave her the power to free herself from the past. "Oh, Lord! What have I done?! What must I do now?!" Bracing herself at the sink, hands gripping the edge, looking and darting her eyes around the room, she dared to look at herself in the mirror, the light fading. The visage of her power looked directly at her. Candelaria swiftly drew away to go out into the other room.

CHAPTER FIVE

The last thing Jim heard when he left his mother's house that day before the viewing, was her sharp command, "Be back by four! Four p.m.!" He drove away in a hurry, anxious to see his grandmother's burned house. Stopping first at the barn, he parked his sedan, grabbed a pitchfork and shovel, placing them in the back of the pickup truck. He put on his coveralls and heavy work boots, then stuffed a pair of work gloves into his back pocket.

His apprentice, a boy who was the blacksmith's adopted son, busily cleaned the stalls, spreading fresh hay and feeding the horses. Jim got in his truck and, before driving away, told the boy, "I'm going over to my grandma's to clean up all the mess. It might take me awhile, so you're in charge until Walt gets back. Okay, Johnny?"

The boy excitedly nodded his head. This added responsibility was important enough to give him a good excuse why he missed school, so he was doubly grateful. He stood a little taller, checking around the barn to be sure everything was in order, because he was in charge. This occasion even required a glimpse in the jagged piece of mirror propped on a shelf, using his fingers to comb his golden brown hair.

When Jim arrived at the house, he set to work on his self-appointed task. He was glad the rain had ceased and wasted no time methodically grabbing junk and tossing it into the back of the truck. He found half-burnt furniture, burnt boards, scorched blankets, pillows, and books, and kitchen items twisted and melted. He told his wife only what everyone else knew, that his grandmother died, he needed to help out his mother, and get back to work. No one besides his apprentice knew where he was until the boy showed up in a second truck driven by Jim's partner, Walter Henry, the blacksmith.

The three of them respected one another for the work they did and the care they gave the horses, which was well known. That respect had its roots in a story of hardship in which they shared. Jim, Walter Henry, and Johnny, each had a mysterious, unspoken past no one talked about for years. It was because of their mutual love and acceptance of one another, that they were bound to confidentiality about each other's private lives, connected by these very secrets.

One trip to the dump accomplished, they returned to load up more. Any relics worth saving were tossed into a box for Jim to take to his mother. Although, there was one item he strained to find even in the soggiest, ash-strewn muck. It was his football medal, last seen where it lovingly draped a small scrapbook of his grandmother's. Grabbing and tossing, shoveling and flinging the soggy black debris and charred clothing into the two trucks, he desperately searched for the medal. He believed it proved his worth, providing concrete evidence that there was yet hope.

Walter Henry raked and tidied, telling Jim, "You better leave 'fore you're late getting back to your mom's. We'll take what's left to the dump."

Disheartened and more disappointed than anyone could imagine, Jim slid the box of his finds onto the floor of the truck cab. He drove one last time to the dump and unloaded everything. Exhausted, he walked around the truck to get in, unexpectedly feeling his emotions. He leaned against the cab, burying his face in his arms. His tears were given no chance to run. His temper flared, a gloved fist pounded the side of the vehicle and, with a hasty scrub of his sleeve across his eyes, he climbed in and drove away. Eventually, he made his way home, relieved his wife was at work, and proceeded to get a bath. Stepping into the bathtub, he slipped a little, but caught himself. A morbid thought came over him as he sank into the warm water, frightening him. He shook it off and was soon bathed, dressed in jeans and a t-shirt. Before returning to his mother's house, he decided to put on a respectable, Sunday shirt.

Walter Henry and his son surveyed their clean-up job. Other than the burnt branches of trees too close to the fire, what remained were some pipes and items still usable, a toilet, a pedestal sink, a bathtub, and odds and end tools, sure to be scavenged over time. An abandoned outhouse stood unharmed a short distance away in the trees.

The boy found a pair of glasses and hid them, at first, but decided to show them to his father. With his face scrunched up in hopeful disappointment, he begged, "Can I have these?"

Walter Henry debated whether to let the boy keep them, but figured it was okay. "Sure. Why not?" He was a tall, lanky man with gray hair and mustache, wearing overalls. He looked fondly upon his boy whose life was a little bit happier once he put the glasses on and looked around.

Ev's grandfather, Timoteo Garcia, was their original owner. Besides clothing and a few personal items, they were the only possession Ev's mother had left to her name. Climbing aboard the wagon back in 1865, she tucked them in the pocket of her skirt, looking over her shoulder toward where her parent's cabin once stood. A stone fireplace and chimney was all that remained. Like a bared and unprotected sentinel, it stood, alone in a green field. Its stones were hauled from miles away using a wagon drawn by a prized pair of mules, a story now lost, along with Timoteo's life.

Johnny soon tired of the heirloom pair of glasses that survived two house fires. For now, he set them on a board next to the broken mirror in the barn. Other such treasures were placed here he would in time forget, though would one day rediscover, a few old marbles, a small horse made of china, and one or two playing dice. One piece he was not about to set in a dusty barn, for it was far too prized a find, was a small, slender, leather-bound scrapbook, the very same one Jim's medal once adorned. Johnny found it early on in their work that day. He stuffed it down the front pocket of his overalls, wanting to keep it for himself, though it had its own part to play in the unfolding events further along the road.

•　•　•

Later that day, Jim and his wife ate the food he brought home from his grandmother's viewing. Afterward, he hurried into the living room, nervously announcing, "I need to take care of things at the livery stable."

"Oh," was all Beth said, her mouth rounded between her fleshy cheeks. Bearing a habitual, scornful mistrust of him, she left the kitchen, anxiously following close behind. She turned on the porch light, since it was now dusk.

Annoyed, Jim yanked his head toward her as he grabbed his jacket. *"What?!"* He wanted to get away. He was craving the woman he was seeing and knew Beth was suspicious, even jealous, so he calmed down and lied to her, "I won't be gone that long." Hurrying out the door and down the porch steps, he went around the house to the path leading over to the barn. He let out a sharp whistle and called, "Shep! Tessie!" Two German Shepherds dashed out from an opening under the porch, eager to join him.

Beth scurried outside and, like a guard whose prisoner has given them the slip, frantically looked on after her husband, watching him walk away into the night. Running her fingers through her wild mop of blond hair, she groaned and shrieked simultaneously. "He's going to see *her!*"

When Jim arrived at the barn, the dogs ran ahead, barking at someone backed up against the workbench with their hands up by their chin. Jim yelled at the dogs again. Surprised to see it was Forty Sumner, Jim almost let out a word he would regret, but instead grabbed the dogs, saying, "It's okay. You know Forty," and pet them. Soon, they ran off to chase after little rustlings coming from the hay, so Jim's unexpected visitor finally relaxed.

"What can I do for you, Forty?"

Jim could barely hide how annoyed he was by his neighbor's unwelcome presence. He wondered why Walter Henry allowed the man to stay. Frustrated, he decided to close up the barn for the day. While he did so, he tried not to think about Forty's wife, Sylvia, whom he planned to meet that evening.

An incident in recent days tipped off Forty's detective nature. The last time he and Jim encountered one another, Jim cast his eyes upon Forty's wife, even made comments to her he found inappropriate. Earlier, he arrived home from work and heard his wife on the phone with someone named Jim. He admired Jim Hart, dreaded the thought of suspecting the town's hero, but he made up his mind to confront the man. Reminding himself that any husband would do the same, and every detective would fearlessly track down any clues that appeared, he approached his suspect.

Running his fingertips across his belly until he found his navel, he said, "Well, I . . ."

Trying not to laugh, Jim acted without hesitation. "Say! Forty! I've been needing to talk to you."

"You—you have?" Surprised, Forty followed Jim out of the barn, eagerly awaiting his possible confession. The detective, he reminded himself, always let the other man do the talking.

Securing the lock on the front door, Jim casually mentioned, "You know what? I saw Jim Stewart with your wife the other day."

Instantly alert, Forty scrambled to think what Chester Ferguson would do. He decided to feign innocence. "Is that so?"

"I saw him parked at your house."

"That can't be!" Forty shouted, disbelieving the other man. "Stewart doesn't drive! He doesn't even own a car!"

Jim nonchalantly replied, "He must have borrowed it."

Forty recalled his wife saying, only recently, that Stewart delivered their groceries, as a favor, while he was at work! "Goodbye, Jim!" Forty dashed away.

Bitterly disappointed in himself, Jim went back inside the barn, retrieving a small bottle of whiskey he hid in a barrel. Pulling up a stool lying on its side by the work bench, he sat and drank until there was no more left. After a long while, with Sylvia and his plans forgotten, he climbed up to the loft and lay down.

Shep and Tessie lingered outside the barn, whining and milling about in the dark until they gave up and left for home. Pine Way fell silent. In the illusory quietude of the evening, their master was now alone.

The moon rose above the mountain ridge in the east while a great rush of air swept over the barn. The building shuddered with its sudden force. Pine cones thudded with a bang and then another bang onto the roof. Dozing, Jim awoke, listening to the pine cones rattling their way across the shingles. The sudden flutter of feathers announced the owls were positioning themselves to set out on their hunting foray across the fields. Emotions Jim stifled with drink, haunted him, regardless. Like a hot iron laid on his back, they seared into his awareness with relentless judgement.

Wishing his father was still alive, he spoke softly in his growing languor, "I miss you, Dad." Faintly rekindling old arguments, he felt remorseful, wanting only to love his father. "I'm sorry." Memories filtered through the darkness, sifting into his mind, like dust. Settling between the layers of time, they began lifting like pages torn and blown away. Down into the valley, they flew, into the night, into the past, sweeping into one scene, his father and a woman at the stables where they worked together. Jim never told his mother what he saw. Now, he wept, grieving the greater loss of family, not knowing how to heal, how to bring back a sense of wholeness, how to mend what lay broken so long ago. Stretching one of his arms, his shirt sleeve drew upward, exposing the scars on his wrist to the moonlight peering between the cracks of boards.

CHAPTER SIX

On the porch of her little shack, Candelaria sat, immersed in a world of words and song and story. Furiously, she wrote, the words pouring from her pen. Tears ran unhindered down her cheeks. Her chest heaved from sobbing, her movements rhythmically rocking her forward and back to her quiet humming.

No one paid her any notice. The sun lowered in the sky and the day's activities subsided for the evening. Crickets cheeped and bleeped and chirruped. Bats roosting by day, set forth, swooping and flitting around edges of trees, sparkling wet from rain. Wind blew through pine and oak, gently whirring in a breathless rushing, sending heavy water droplets splattering earthward. Rays of sunlight shone from beneath departing clouds, becoming misty beams of golden light.

Candelaria was finally at peace. The storm within herself found its outlet. Gazing upon the fields and orchards beyond, a vision appeared, a man walking through tall grass between the orchard trees as though in a dream. He turned, walking toward her, holding a stem of grass between his fingers. Someone Candelaria thought familiar, his face almost registered in her mind. The vision gently faded, as mysteriously as it appeared, leaving her in awe, seeking an explanation for what she witnessed. Returning her gaze toward the field again, she hoped the scene might return. A voice, calling to her repeatedly, broke her concentration.

"Laria! Laria!"

She startled.

It was her neighbor, who cried, "What did you do to your hair?!" The woman drew her arm around Candelaria, knowing it was the grief. She asked if she could help her clean the house.

Candelaria replied, "Yeah! Sure!"

She grabbed the notebook and pen and went indoors to place them on her dresser. In the mirror, she saw her smeared mascara, so she washed her face and blew her nose. Her hair! It was horrible! Drying her face with the towel, she decided to stop wearing make-up. Her mother often told her, "You're too pretty for make-up, Laria. Don't wear that nonsense. You don't need it!"

Sweeping the bathroom floor, she sensed this day marked the beginning of a series of important changes in her life. Unsure of what they might entail, she bravely acknowledged her days of hiding had come to an end. It was time for her to expand and grow beyond her limited life. A frightening prospect, to her, though fully aware she could not return to whom she was before her mother died. Wherever she was headed, she was already on her way. Whatever changes lay ahead, they were already taking place. They were already happening.

Meanwhile, the neighbor woman who came over to help her, managed to get the food put away, making sure to set aside a couple platefuls for herself to take home. Someone brought spareribs, of which she was especially fond, and even some tamales. Everything smelled so good! She walked the few steps toward the little living room.

Candelaria lay on the sofa staring at the television, watching the news, her face flashing lighter and dimmer, scenes changing before her in the otherwise unlit room. She was exhausted. Protective of her newfound self, she savored the change, basking in a waking dream. Joy and opportunities were open to her since the discovery of her gifts.

The woman, leaning against the doorway and resting her head, spoke quietly to Candelaria, whom she knew since they were in elementary school. She was a couple of years older and always felt like a big sister to this one. Candelaria was her best friend. Her eyes became moist with tears, her heart burning with love for this woman who endured so much. Her lips quivered. "Life," she wondered, "what is it all about? Why does this one have to suffer?" Turning away, she pushed her ample weight away from the doorframe, rubbed her eyes and shook her curly black hair, dismissing those thoughts from her mind.

"Good night, Larie," she said, and prepared to leave, collecting the food-laden plates.

Candelaria called out to her, "Chavie."

It was barely loud enough, yet the woman heard. It was a nickname not spoken since girlhood, for her maiden name, Chavez.

Insistent, Candelaria raised her voice, saying, "Chavie!"

Esther Gutierrez, which was her married name, walked timidly toward the living room. She set the plates down and answered, "Yeah? What?" The name brought to her awareness that her girlhood feelings still lived within her. They were stirred, giving her a sense of independence and daring, strength and fearlessness. She stepped into the living room and looked at the woman lying on the sofa, eyes closed, hair chopped and butchered, and listened to her.

"Chavie, do you remember what it was like at school, what people called us?"

Of course, Esther remembered, but it was Chavie who answered, "Damn right, I do!"

Candelaria began to cry again. "We never did anything about it. We just took it!"

Esther's heart melted, her own tears once again breaking through, ready to agree with her friend, quietly and humbly, as though defeated. "No, we didn't, Larie. We just took it."

Candelaria's eyes opened. She told her friend what she wanted to do, to drive to the state capital to make a stand with the other Chicanos, like she saw on the news.

Esther inquired, "Chicanos?" She failed to grasp its meaning, but Chavie knew and pushed Esther aside. "Let's go!"

They devised a plan to go in Esther's car, bringing the food with them. Esther went home, emboldened to act, determined to follow through with it. What her husband would say was another thing. She recalled him mentioning some people coming to talk to the pickers, getting them riled. He was against it. She knew as much as she walked toward their own shack. Her husband was waiting, because she promised to bring home some of the food for their dinner. The porch light was on. Swatting away moths and other flying insects, she opened the door to her house. Leaving it open, she entered the small structure, securing the screen door shut.

"Hey, Jorge! I'm home!" No answer, so she yelled again, "George! Hey, I got the food!" Pleased with herself, she added, "and cake, too!"

Squeaky bedsprings sounded from another room. Other noises, yawning and farting, announced Jorge had gotten out of bed. He staggered into the kitchen with his socks flopping around, falling off his feet. His belt was undone, his pants partially unzipped, and he was scratching his messy hair and yawning some more.

An idea came to Esther, "Maybe I'll tell him and maybe I won't."

CHAPTER SEVEN

In need of some helpful advice, Rosa left work earlier that same day to meet with a co-worker friend at Teapot full o' Whimsy. It was the new bakery at the shopping center, which several men in town jokingly referred to as "the ladies saloon." Many of its baked goods were "rum-this" or "rum-that," they claimed. What only added fuel to their comedic fire, was that its owner possessed a cherry red nose, which they attributed to her "taking a nip too many from that teapot full o' rum-sy!" Roaring with laughter and slapping one another on the back, they shamelessly reveled in their hilarity. One might even add, "Trudy Price's real name must have been Rudy, short for *Rudolph!*" The jokesters, who never seemed to have any work to do, might amble over to the hardware store, the barber shop, or the diner. Never mind their teasing, women loved the new bakery with its brightly colored tablecloths, decorative shelving, and character teapots and cookie jars. Rosa was no exception. She and her friend, Dottie, were frequent customers, when Rosa could afford it.

Dottie was already seated at their favorite spot by the window. Plenty of wrought-iron tables and chairs, which were painted white, furnished the place, but she preferred to sit at the wobbly one, because it afforded the best view of people walking by outside. While sipping their tea, they commented on recent events of small importance. Dottie secretly desired to share a little bit of news she could hardly contain. She nonchalantly drank her tea, the other arm with elbow resting on the table, hand poised as if she was modeling. No longer able to withhold her latest secret, she suddenly leaned toward Rosa and, lowering her voice, said, "You won't *believe* who I saw coming out of this very beauty parlor next door." Looking out the window, she waited, sipping her tea and pretending to be casual.

Rosa forgot about her friend's gossipy nature. She put herself on guard to choose someone else from whom to seek advice. Nevertheless, she inquired, "Who?" One hand flicked the crumbs from her fingertips onto her plate. "Well...who?"

"*Sylvia Sumner!* Cut off all her hair!" Dottie ignored the fact she was spreading gossip about her own cousin.

Unable to contain herself any longer, Rosa grabbed her purse. Her grandmother died and her emotions reached the spillover point. She hastily said, "I'm sorry, Dottie. I've got to go." Her metal chair went grinding backward along the floor as she stood up to leave. Rushing outside, the doorbell jangled in response. Once in her car, she immediately drove away.

Dottie stared out the bakery window wondering what *that* was all about. She lightly patted her short, blond bouffant hairdo and checked her nail polish, still fresh, deciding she needed to find out more. Her mother owned the other beauty parlor where she and Rosa worked as beauticians. Once she returned to work, her mother told her everything regarding the Hart family's misfortunes and tragic loss. Regretting her earlier behavior at the bakery, Dottie resolved to make amends. Unfortunately, her midafternoon appointment arrived. After what seemed like hours, she was finally free to go. She fixed her pearl pink lipstick, dropped the gold-plated case into her clutch purse and snapped it shut, informing her mother, "I'll be right back."

Her mother, none other than Sylvia Sumner's aunt, was married to Clarence McGrew. He ran the old Forbush's Market until it closed down, then opened the suitcase factory where many of Edenville's citizens worked. He did pretty well by himself and, Patience, who most people knew as "Patty," believed she had also done well. The town's ladies needed a beauty parlor more than she needed the money, so, while it was not busy at Patty's Beautique, she could afford for the girls to come and go as they pleased. She was very proud of the fact that Clarence was a direct descendant of Thomas McGrew, one of Edenville's earliest settlers and the original owner of the Pine Way General Store. It was his house they lived in until the suitcase factory began to boom. She often said, "Keep on travelin', people! My husband and I *love* the money!" Drawing a section of her customer's hair into the air between her fingertips and snipping away, she repeated it, quietly chuckling to herself regarding her wit.

Near closing time, Rosa timidly entered the salon, her eyes red and a bit puffy.

Patty gently scolded her. "What are you doin' here, girl? You should be with your mother." Her scissored hand pointed back to the door and a jerk of her head joined it. "Now go on and get out of here."

Rosa had no place else to go except to work. Nevertheless, her distracted state of mind rendered her unfit to be cutting people's hair. She turned to leave. Truth is, she avoided going home, imagining her grandmother's corpse on display, right where they watched television, and in the same room where she slept every night! She pretended to follow Patty's advice. Her pale yellow, short-sleeved blouse ill-prepared her for a chilly day that was growing colder. She draped her light-green sweater closer about her shoulders, buttoning only the top button, and smoothed her lime green capri pants before walking across the street toward her gray Chevy four-door. At times like these, when Rosa needed comforting, she usually turned to her grandmother. She would lay down and place her head on her grandmother's lap, her hair gently caressed as they talked privately. But, Grandma Ev was gone.

Burdened with various issues, Rosa began weighing her choices, appearing to wander aimlessly along the sidewalk past her car. Checking to see if anyone was looking, she abruptly stepped off the sidewalk, slipping behind the buildings between the diner and the barber shop. She went directly toward the back entrance of the hardware store. She knew the young man who worked in the plumbing department. Hand raised, she knocked on the door using their special signal, two quick raps followed by one quiet knock.

Dottie McGrew, who was still looking for Rosa, spotted her going behind the diner, so she ran to catch up to her, calling out her name. But, Rosa continued entering the hardware store, leaving the door ajar behind her. In less than a minute, Dottie pulled the door open, shocked to find her best friend, standing there in the back room of Goodman's Hardware Store kissing Buster Smith! Buster's hands dropped and he and Rosa parted. In dismay, Dottie glanced from one guilty party to the other before she turned around and fled out the back door, wanting only to get away. Crying unreservedly, she ran to the beauty parlor, Rosa close behind.

"Dottie! Stop! Wait!"

One shoe fell off Rosa's foot. She hastily picked it up and kept running, yelling, "Dottie! Please, wait!" Her dark brown hair blew in the wind. Her shoe and bare foot became dirty and wet from running carelessly along the path through the dampened grass.

Dottie halted and burst out, "How *could* you?! You know how much I've liked him!" Her face was pinched in an angry pout.

Rosa tried explaining, "I'm sorry, Dottie, but Buster and I are in love!"

"In *love?!*" Dottie was incredulous, not knowing if laughter or more yelling was going to come out of her mouth next. It seemed ridiculous. In love? Love was an unknown to her. Her charms and pretending to be grown up and womanly were all she knew.

She wanted her mother, yet was terribly ashamed of herself. Trying to be a good friend, she apologized, "I'm sorry, Rosa," she said while hugging her. "Earlier, at the bakery, I-I should have been more thoughtful about you losing your grandmother and her house burning down. I'm really sorry."

Having nothing more to say, except to mumble a soft goodbye, Dottie turned and walked around to the end of the buildings, then across the street toward the beauty salon. Somehow, she had shrunk in stature, thinking of herself as a little, lost girl, dressed up for a party no one will attend. The town square seemed too quiet and empty. Where was everybody? Stepping inside the beauty parlor, she hurried over to her mother.

"Oh, Mommy!" Dottie sank into her mother's open arms and cried like a young girl.

"Goodness, gracious, Dottie." Wondering what more their emotional day could have wrought, Patty asked her, "What's the matter?"

"I feel so stupid! I'm so ashamed!" Through her crying, Dottie shared Rosa and Buster's news.

Patty was not surprised. She hugged her daughter again. "Let's go home, okay?"

The bell jangled one last time. Dottie waited beside the curb for her mother, anxiously hoping to see her friend before leaving to go home. She wanted to give a conciliatory wave to Rosa, but needed to forego the gesture once her mother started up the car.

Her mother soon drove them home in Dottie's own automobile. Her parents may have given her the two-door Dodge coupe, a bright, opalescent blue, her favorite color, for her twenty-first birthday, but she long suspected they purchased the car for themselves. Growing ashamed of such an extravagant gift, she decided to stop making a fuss and let them have the car.

Rosa neared the sidewalk as Dottie and her mother drove away, realizing she embarked on something new. Choosing to step across the threshold placed before her, she lost something dear in the process, leaving it behind. It reminded her of when she became a teenager and had a similar, life-changing experience. Her mother had suddenly become an embarrassment to her and fell from on high into someone limited and ordinary. After that challenging day, Rosa never wanted to be like her, instead striving to improve herself and her prospects in life. Unknowingly, at the time, what she lost in the process was her girlhood.

Her feet felt cold and wet. Looking down, she saw her socks and shoes, soaking wet and dirty. Impractical, yet inexpensive canvas sneakers she bought at the five and dime, now seemed to her an extravagant and wasteful purchase, something she needed to curtail in the future. With eyes on the ground before her, she walked toward her car in the dimming light, unaware of crickets singing and bats swooping, or even sunsets, like the remarkable one taking place that evening.

Many of Edenville's citizens lingered on their porches to watch the sun silently melt into the trees. Like crayons left to lie in the hot sun, the colors peach and magenta, aqua and violet ran together into crimson blood, letting the night come with soft memory for all those in attendance. Gradually, darkness swallowed the blazing fire of day's end.

• • •

Patty McGrew announced, "I think there's gonna be a wedding in that family real soon." She chuckled, having observed Rosa occasionally leave the beauty parlor for lunch at the same time Buster Smith left the hardware store.

Patty knew Buster's family all his life. A good family, two boys, with Buster being the eldest. His real name was Stephen Bertram Smith, but he frequently got into trouble with their next-door neighbor, Justice Walker, who was Patty's sister. Justice shouted after him, "Listen here, Buster!" The name kind of stuck. He got into a fight at school, punched in the mouth. One of his front teeth was chipped by the other boy's fist. When Buster talked too fast, he whistled a little, so he always tried to talk slow and careful. Sometimes, younger kids intentionally riled him, so they could hear him yell and whistle at the same time. "Hey! Get over here, you punksth!" He chased after them, yelling, "I'm gonna kick your asthsth!" The kids ran off like "thieving little rapscallions," according to Justice, from their entire day basically "running loose like a pack of coyotes," she often remarked.

Even though her sister's rendition was not meant to be humorous, Patty giggled at the remembrance of it. When she parked on their wraparound driveway at their house on the hill overlooking the valley, she smiled to herself, knowing exactly what she could do for Rosa and Buster, never mind the cost. Her rationale was, "The good Lord didn't give me all this money, so's I could keep it all to myself!"

Her mumbling caught Dottie's attention. "What did you say, Mommy?"

Patty adored her daughter, affectionately placing her arm around her. Together, they walked up the paved drive to the front door of their four-bedroom, ranch-style home on five acres, complete with swimming pool, sauna, and three-car garage.

She happily shared her ideas, "You and me, girl, are gonna do something very special for Rosa and her family."

Dottie caught on to her mother's joy. "What? Tell me!"

"Well, we've got to make some plans, just you and me, then we've got to share them with Daddy, before we mention any of it to Rosa. Don't tell anyone else 'til we've talked to him okay?"

"All right."

They stepped into the house and waited for Daddy McGrew to get home from work, so they could discuss their latest plan. Before cooking dinner, Patty went into their sunken living room to sit awhile in her recliner and take a short nap, while Dottie went into her pink bedroom, closed the door, and threw herself onto her bed to cry.

CHAPTER EIGHT

Later that evening, Rosa arrived at her and her mother's house. She collected her purse and a paper sack containing various sundry items she purchased at the five and dime. It was only a pack of gum and a new shade of lipstick, plus a notepad made especially for planning a wedding. Cautiously overjoyed, she quelled her excitement until she saw her mother. The house was dark, so she turned on the kitchen light and placed her things on the counter. In a low voice, she called out, "Mom?"

Candelaria was already roused out of bed when she heard Rosa's keys and the screen door slowly creak its way closed. About to rush to the kitchen to greet her daughter and show her the food people brought, she felt her short hair. Anxious, she stopped a minute to rummage through a dresser drawer for a scarf with which to conceal her ravaged scalp.

Rosa was examining the food in the refrigerator, lifting foil wrappers and commenting to herself regarding the savory items she discovered.

Candelaria stepped into the kitchen, nervous and self-conscious about her hair. Rosa looked up and stared with mouth gaping wide.

"Mom! Did you do something to your hair? Did you cut it, or what?"

She closed the refrigerator door and went over to her mother to inspect her hair, but Candelaria held the scarf down with both her hands and skirted around her daughter.

"No, no, no! I don't want you to look. You'll laugh! I know you'll laugh!"

"Mom! What did you do?! Why won't you let me see it?" Rosa made playful attempts at yanking the scarf away until her mother glared at her with a face that appeared unfamiliar and strange. It stunned Rosa. She could tell her mother had been crying, but something else was going on. "Are you okay? What's going on?" Her joyful news drifted away as she became concerned for her mother, not to mention a bit guilty for avoiding coming home earlier. "Tell me, Mom. What's going on? What happened?" Immediately, she remembered her brother was supposed to help out. "Don't tell me, Jim didn't come by to help! Oh, that *brother* of mine!" She rolled her eyes and threw her arms up in the air, as her mother slipped past to get various food items out of the refrigerator.

"Let's see...someone brought tamales and there's some—"

Rosa pulled the scarf off her mother's head before she could be stopped and, instantly, her hand covered her mouth in shock, "Holy—! Mom! What did you do to yourself?!" She was horrified.

"Never mind!" Candelaria replied angrily as she grabbed the scarf out of Rosa's hand. Now defiant, she closed the refrigerator and made a show of sauntering lazily out of the kitchen. "You're a big girl. You can get your own dinner. I need lots of rest cuz

I'm going to the state capital tomorrow to make a stand with my people."

She returned to bed, leaving Rosa to wonder what her mother was planning and what tomorrow would bring.

• • •

The following day, Candelaria took a bath and, while drying her hair afterward, yelled out to Rosa that Esther was due to arrive. She advised her daughter, "If you want to go with us, you'd better get ready!"

Rosa folded the sofa bed, wondering what was so strikingly different about her mother's face. She eyed her mother, sweeping from room to room, until it dawned on her. "Where's your make-up, Mom? Aren't you going to put on any make-up?"

Candelaria ignored her, very casually pulling on a pair of her husband's blue jeans she saved and a white t-shirt, rolling up the sleeves practically to her shoulders, and tucking the shirt into her pants.

Rosa was thoroughly disgusted. Her mother's choppy, butch haircut was bad enough. But, to *dress* like a man, too? *"Mom!"* Absolutely mortified, she pleaded with her mother to stop this nonsense. It completely insulted her beautician's sense of decorum. "You can't be serious! What are you doing dressing up like that?!" She followed closely behind her mother, herself still in her nightgown, scooting about in her fuzzy slippers, cold cream caked all over her face, and her hair set in outrageously large curlers.

Candelaria spun around to face her and, with an air of superiority, looked her daughter up and down. "Have you looked at *yourself* in the mirror lately?" She breezed into the kitchen, proceeding to pack for her day embracing her people as one of their own.

Rosa gave up and plopped down on the sofa, crying. "This was supposed to be the happiest time of my life and you're *ruining* it!" She put her face in her hands to get a really good cry going, but only smeared the cold cream. Angrily, she stormed into the bathroom, washed her face, pulled the curlers out of her hair, then grabbed another pair of her father's old pants. She threw off her nightgown, hopping around trying to pull up the pants. She also put on a t-shirt. With an air of defiance, she stepped into the kitchen, challenging her mother, determined to prove how ridiculous dressing this way appeared. "All *right!* If you're going like that, so am I!"

She stood in the kitchen, her mother looking at her, turning her around and messing her hair, commenting, "Not bad, Rosa." Candelaria burst out laughing and Rosa joined in, both of them in hysterics, when someone knocked at the door.

Candelaria opened it to see her neighbor, Esther, dressed like she was going to church, wearing a yellow-and-white cotton dress, white belt and gloves, nylon stockings, and heels, and a matching hat. She even wore her hair curled.

Esther stood on their porch, slightly glaring at the two of them, and said, "I'm sorry. I think I'm at the wrong house. Two ladies supposedly live here." Quickly, she turned around to walk away, wagging her head in disapproval, then swiftly turned back, saying, "My, my, my." With her purse handle slipped over her wrist, she turned on them, all Chavie. "Let me tell you something! When you go somewhere important, to stand with *your people*, you are *proud* of who you are!" She looked them over with scorn in her eyes. "This looks to me more like just a game, like some kind of joke to you two."

Chastised and humbled, Candelaria and Rosa grew serious. Candelaria was disappointed in herself. She knew her friend was right. She changed her clothes, realizing the best way to behave was neither subservient nor defiant, but proud, respectful, and kind.

While Esther finished packing some of the food in a grocery sack, Rosa changed into something she usually wore to church.

Someone came to the doorway, looked into the kitchen, and yelled, "Ma! When are we going?!" It was Esther's daughter, Socorro Alvarez, who dropped out of high school when she got pregnant and, afterward, got married. She was only a year or two older than Rosa, but had three kids in school. Her mother asked her to drive them, because her father needed their car.

Ecstatic, Rosa greeted her friend, "Coco! Are you coming, too?!"

"Are you kidding? Who'd wanna miss this?!"

Soon, they began filing out the door, ready to go, when Candelaria crept out of her room, weeping and lovingly stroking her butchered hair, pouting, "My hair! My beautiful hair!" She looked so pathetic, everyone hugged her.

Rosa took pity on her mother and knew exactly what she needed. She pronounced loudly, "Quick trip to Patty's Beautique!"

Once they got into the car and drove off, Candelaria recalled her daughter's words. "What did you mean, Rosa, saying this was supposed to be the happiest time of your life?"

Rosa dismissed it with a quick sweeping gesture of her hand through the air. "Later, Mom. I'll tell you later."

At the beauty parlor, Patty insisted on doing Candelaria's hair. Trimmed and evened out, curled and hair-sprayed, a smile returned to Candelaria's face. She even agreed to a little bit of make-up, knowing this was an important day, not just for them, but for all Mexican-Americans. Considering the truth, tears welled up in her eyes. She felt proud! "I *am* an American," she realized," a *Mexican*-American!"

CHAPTER NINE

It was a long drive from their small mountain valley to their destination. After climbing the slope to the west, the highway descended into the immense valley beyond. It was usually hot or buried beneath a thick layer of fog. Sometimes, it flooded from heavy, torrential winter rains.

Their trip brought memories to Candelaria as they drove on in silence. "Too many people," her mother used to murmur to herself, her eyes fixed on the scenery rushing past the window. She never hesitated letting Candelaria know how much she disliked going to the doctor.

Rosa and Coco were in the front seat, exchanging tidbits of news about their lives since they last saw one another.

"Where're your kids?" Rosa asked, because this would be a long day.

Coco, who was so short, she could barely see over the top of the steering wheel, replied casually, "Oh, my mother-in-law's taking care of them. They have fun together. It'll be okay."

"How about you?" Alluding to Rosa and Buster's news, Coco ventured, "I heard something about you and—"

Rosa placed her hand on Coco's arm, signaling her not to say any more, so they ended up not talking, either.

Candelaria looked out the window. Her gaze wandered past farms with worn-out houses and broken-down, rusted cars. Chickens and goats clamored in ramshackle pens. Laundry hanging to dry, swiftly set sail, waving and flapping in the breeze. The rain left the days cooler, but the sky was clear and bright blue. She remembered accompanying her husband on work-related trips. In fact, the last time she saw him was on one such excursion. He apprenticed with his father to be a blacksmith, but he made it his specialty to board and care for horses. This specialty led him to become a farrier. He was known everywhere as one of the best. Horse breeders and owners of big racehorse stables called on him, so much so, their family considered moving. She remembered her father got sick and Jim's problems started to make themselves known. The move was no longer discussed. It was simply forgotten. Still, her husband worked in the valley, sometimes being gone all week long. He taught their son everything he knew.

She wondered if the racehorse stables relied on her son the way they once counted on her husband. Feeling bad, she realized she rarely noticed what he did for work. Since her husband died, her fears and worries, her newfound vulnerability and uncertainty over the future, dominated her perspective. It dawned on her, that she turned to her son to fill his father's shoes, instead of going to college on his football scholarship. They were so proud of him!

She stopped those thoughts, not wanting to dwell on the mistakes she had made, but she told herself to ask Jim about work. Men appreciated it, she believed. Would it be her place? Did Beth do that? Was she even any good for him?

Her son and his wife lived in the old family home. It originally belonged to her mother-in-law's parents, and was one of the first homesteads established in Pine Way, among the first in their valley. Candelaria's mother-in-law grew the most beautiful garden that was the envy of everyone. Besides roses, she tended wisteria vines, many varieties of bulbs, and vegetables, too. When her in-laws moved away, Candelaria and her husband got the house. He had to work and Candelaria began working with the fruit pickers. Gradually, the garden withered.

Her mother made sure to express her disapproval. "Laria. Tsk, tsk, tsk." She walked amongst the dying garden, hands clasped behind her, looking down toward the ground as if in contemplation, like she always did while out walking.

Candelaria had no clue why she was uninterested in keeping a garden. Not long after her husband died and Jim married, she and Rosa moved into Villa Boracho, the farmworkers' housing. They worked full time, doing whatever they could. Rosa saved her money and went to beauty college. She worked very hard. Candelaria was proud of her.

She recalled Rosa mentioning something. "Rosa? What was it you were saying earlier? Tell me, Rosalita." Rosa's childhood name had not been used in a long time. Candelaria was dressed nice, a new haircut, a new *life*, by golly! She was determined to be a better mother to her children.

Defeated, Rosa told them the latest, expecting them to be disappointed in her. "Buster asked me to marry him. You might as well know, I said, yes." Everyone looked surprised.

Esther-Chavie piped up, "*Buster?!* Why would you want to marry *him*? He's got bad teeth and talks funny. No one respects him! You ought to get a man people respect!"

Esther crossed the line and hurt Rosa's feelings. She burst out crying, demanding Coco stop the car and take her home. She yelled, "Turn around right now!" She repeatedly stamped the floor of the car with both feet and shook herself, like she was having a tantrum.

Candelaria turned on Esther. "Esther! My *gawd!* Who do you think you are, criticizing my daughter that way?! Just look at your fat and sloppy husband!"

Esther shot her a look, but it was Chavie who said the final word as Coco pulled off the highway onto the dirt shoulder. "No one is going home until we do what we came here to do! That's final! If you've got anything more to say, it can wait. We're just nervous. We don't—" She let it go. Tightly hugging her huge purse resting on her big lap, she looked away out the car window, then back again, nodding her head in sharp affirmation. She was determined to lead them onward. Her mind was set.

Coco reached over and patted Rosa's hand, offering her congratulations. Candelaria leaned forward, placing one hand on the front car seat as she lightly patted her daughter's hair and shoulder, saying, "I'm proud of you, Rosa. You'll make a good wife. Buster's a kind man."

She spoke so softly, Rosa barely heard, but she stopped crying and her anger subsided.

Resuming their drive, Coco tried to steer the car back onto the road, but it began sliding into the ditch. She kept the car moving forward, tires spinning and mud flying out from beneath. Fortunately, they finally caught enough traction, she was able to get the car back onto the pavement. Everyone breathed a sigh of relief. After a bit, she turned on the radio. The song playing was about going to the Chapel of Love. Grinning, everyone turned to look at one another. Rosa drew her wedding planner notepad out of her purse and, tenderly, she showed it to Coco. Coco glanced at it and promised she would help Rosa with everything.

Candelaria saw the wedding planner, but said nothing. Both her children marrying further away from her heritage, becoming more like their father and his family, she lamented. This left her feeling alone. She was unsure how it happened, but she knew it was going to be easier for Rosa than it had been for her family. Reminded of her son, she grew concerned and deeply saddened. Not only the garden, but the house itself was in wrack and ruination. In her disappointment, she muttered bitterly to herself, "I could huff and puff and blow that thing down, myself." Beth worked full time and apparently had no interest in taking care of things or even staying in touch with their family. It was a strange situation Candelaria tried not to notice.

Her own family came from Mexico long ago. At least, it was Mexico before some battle took place. Her great-grandfather fought in that battle, named Timoteo Garcia, she recalled. He fought to keep their rightfully owned land. They farmed the rich soil along the river floodplains. Her maternal grandmother, Estefana Garcia, their "Mama Stefa," told her the story when she was a little girl. She remembered it was at their house, where she and her brothers and sister lived with everyone, including her grandmother. One day, when the grass in the fields was green and tall, her grandmother sat them down. One of Candelaria's brothers fell asleep beside the dog as Mama Stefa told the story.

"We are Mexicans and we are storytellers." She looked from one child to the next to be sure they were listening to her, before she continued her story. "To be Mexican is to be a people of both the land and the sun, both native Indio and Spaniard, watching and listening, storytellers of the heart and of the spirit."

Candelaria remembered becoming enraptured by her grandmother's voice, carried off in a dream, traveling where she travelled, soaring where she flew, and seeing what she saw. She remembered the story well, but there were elements she could not know, for her grandmother never told her.

•   •   •

Long ago, Timoteo Garcia made his stand on the land bordering a great, wide river. He lost the fight along with many others, friends and neighbors, family members. Some remained and subjugated themselves to serving these new landowners. Some moved further south into Old Mexico, risking everything. Others, like Timoteo, went northward and entered a vast plain where shaggy beasts overwhelmed these humble folk. They wanted to build houses, not sod huts. They saw the weakening stacks of prairie earth cave in from heavy rains, collapsing on the people huddled within, killing their babies. Most of them walked, some rode, while the lucky ones with carts and wagons, pulled by strong oxen or little burros, travelled until they reached another great river. Here, there were trees. They helped one another to fell the trees and build log houses. Others residing alongside the river taught them how.

Timoteo was alone. He had not married, had no one but himself, and worked hard to saw and cut and shape the wood. Working with the wood, it came to him he had a gift. He would be a carpenter. Bent over his work, he looked out the corner of his eye toward the sky. "Like El Señor," he thought aloud. "Eh, Lord?" He took off his hat and wiped the sweat from his forehead.

One woman, who lost her husband, began to pay him special attention. She made tortillas by the fire in their encampment, but wanted to learn to bake bread like the farm women. They gave her some of their bread from time to time. She would take it to Timoteo, telling him she baked it. He was a good man, and strong, too. She wanted to impress him.

Timoteo knew the truth and yet smiled at her, thanking her. Eventually, the cabin was completed, so he took the young widow as his wife. Her name was Josefa Candelaria Bustamante.

The babies did not come right away, so they assumed they might never have children. After what seemed like an eternity, they were at last blessed with a baby boy, Jose Timoteo de Jesus Garcia, named after his father. Another boy arrived and, years later, they were finally given a daughter, Maria Estefana Garcia. Timoteo taught his sons his trade, showing them how the wood needed to be loved and cared for, like a woman, he thought to himself, caressed and rubbed smooth with oil, he often mused.

Sadly, the two boys died. Fever struck and neighbors were taken ill, faces and skin blotchy red, sweating and weakness, then death. First, the younger boy died and, then, Jose Timoteo. Maddened by this one's death, his wife would not let him be buried, holding him to her, rocking and moaning. Timoteo got others to help him restrain his wife while they pulled the boy's body away from her. Fitfully, she scrabbled in the leaves and dirt outside near the stream, grunting and shrieking, clawing and biting. Once they hurriedly carried the boy away, she threw herself to the ground, wailing in her grief. One woman rushed to hold her, trying to calm her. Their daughter, Estefana, a girl of ten years, was sent to live with her aunt and uncle for a time. She never returned to her mother and father.

Men would come. Guerrillas, they were called, in larger and larger groups of horsemen carrying lit torches and descending upon homes. Some were remote at first. Becoming emboldened by their growing numbers and their soldiers' uniforms, they began attacking entire towns, burning everything, killing everyone they could find. They plundered people's homes, gunning down whole families who tried to fight them. They set fire to Timoteo's log cabin, the torches smashing through their new windows, which had been shipped from the East, arriving packed in crates. In their panic, Timoteo and his wife stayed in their house too long, his wife frantically looking for Estefana, having forgotten she lived elsewhere. Others were yelling for them to get out. Timoteo pulled on his wife to make her leave. Tragically, both of them burned in the fire when the roof caved in and the logs fell in on top of them.

Despite the terror of the horsemen and the screaming of women and children, Estefana ran to her parent's home. Like a strange and vivid dream, she saw inside the house, everything alight, the colors and patterns of fabric seen clearly and her mother and father grabbing hold of one another as the roof toppled. She screamed. Her aunt and uncle ran to her, catching her as she fell toward the ground. Going into hysterics, her uncle managed to pick her up and carry her away from the horrors of the night.

The survivors camped beside a stream. Those whose homes had been spared, aided those who lost their homes. All were fed. All received care. Estefana lived with her aunt and uncle until the following year, when it was time for them to leave. They were going back to Mexico, they said, and placed her in the care of another family heading west, the Walker's, who promised to keep her safe. Withdrawn and silent as though she were yet in a state of shock, she was lifted onto the wagon and left for the West, along with other emigrants, many like refugees fleeing bloodshed and hatred.

•　　•　　•

Candelaria remembered feeling so far away as her grandmother told the story, her voice like a lulling wind sweeping through the pines. Candelaria's big brother peacefully slept in the tall grass, the dog panting and then stretching, looking for something else to do. The spell would be broken. Not wanting it to end, she laid her head in her grandmother's lap, begging for her to sing a particular song that she loved. Like a peaceful, calming dream, her grandmother sang softly in Spanish, gently tugging on strands of Candelaria's hair and combing it with her fingers.

That special time in her life was taken for granted and, now, so many years ago, it seemed like another life. The house that was built by her father, Jesse Mendoza, burned to the ground, and her mother's valued possessions contained within were now lost. Previously, she mentioned wanting to dig through the remains of the house. Rosa told her, a little untruthfully, she had already done so and found only a couple of items she promised to show her when they returned home.

Candelaria leaned forward and placed a hand on the top of the front seat to ask Coco, "Are we almost there?" Coco only replied, no, but they would arrive soon. Candelaria was tired, closing her eyes and dozing off to sleep as Esther had done, wanting to get there already, though unsure of what they might see.

CHAPTER TEN

That same morning, Walter Henry arrived at work to hear Jim up in the loft. He feared the young man had company. "Jim's carryin' on with that Sumner woman again," he grumbled. His angry assumption led to concern for Johnny's welfare. He signaled to the boy with a nod of his head to get back in the truck. It was bad enough he kept quiet and avoided the issue, but he refused to expect his son to do the same.

Seeing Johnny's sour, brooding face, Walter Henry decided to treat the boy to a second breakfast before school started. Parking in front of Millie's Kitchen, immediately enlivened the boy's spirits, especially once they entered the diner. They each ordered the largest breakfast selection on the menu, blueberry pancakes with a side of maple sausage, hash browns, scrambled eggs with cheese, coffee, and hot chocolate with whipped cream for the boy. They ate everything with gusto.

Millie stood by, watching Johnny lick his plate clean. She was tickled, and secretly loved the boy, wanting to lift him up in her arms and hug him, and take away all his worries. She thought he was the saddest poor boy she had ever seen. Others gathered around, laughing and applauding. Walter Henry even paid cash, she was quick to note.

"Thank you, Walter."

Privately, she held in her heart a secret love for the old gentleman, but he was not interested, she believed. Dressed in her pink and white, starched, freshly pressed uniform with a white cap, white shoes for people on their feet all day, she gave them a wink and a smile.

"You take care, now."

They slightly staggered out the door, much too skinny to run out of eating room. One man looked on, also smiling. He was not skinny, but he ate his meals with a ravenous zeal. Millie never minded. Sam Goodman was, well, a good man. He ran the hardware store, situated next to her diner, so he was a frequent visitor.

Sam was looking out the window, as one viewing a scene from the past. Keeping his voice low, and fishing in his pocket for a tip to leave by his plate, he said, "I wonder how ol' Lulabelle's doin'."

"I don't know, Sam," Millie said. "Don't see her anymore."

Millie had her hands on her hips, noticing the breakfast crowd gradually departing. She needed to get to work on her lunch items. "Let's see," she said to herself, while walking briskly into the kitchen. "Monday, that was yesterday. My ham and bean soup— Oh! That was Turkey Sandwich Day." Merely as a side joke, she sometimes made it a cold turkey sandwich, for those who imbibed a little too much over the weekend and needed to lay off the stuff for the week ahead.

When she made hot turkey sandwiches, she used fresh bread from the bakery, nice and soft, fresh mashed potatoes and gravy, lots of it, too. She included a dollop of homemade cranberry sauce, sometimes canned. It always included her special sweet potato pecan pie à la mode with a drizzle of caramel sauce. "Just a tad," she told customers.

Millicent May Forester loved feeding people. She never married, though longed for it, never had children, either. Something no living person knew, was that she got pregnant when she was a teenager. Her family lived in Pine Way at the time. She and a neighbor boy spent a lot of time together that did not involve playing checkers. Both families were ashamed. Her parents speedily arranged for Millie to live with distant relatives until she had the baby.

However, the pregnancy abruptly concluded in a miscarriage, so she never left. Regardless, the boy's family packed up and moved, telling no one where they were going. Millie was not especially scarred from the experience. It never became known to anyone else in town, that she knew. More than anything, it left her maternally hungering. She babysat every child she could and volunteered at children's events. Eventually, she discovered cooking. She cooked for the Spring Hill Residence & Infirmary for many years, diligently saving her money until she bought the diner, well into her forties by then.

The diner was somewhat of a tourist attraction in wintertime, with people traveling to ski resorts and families heading up to play in the snow. She earned a reputation and even garnered a little bit of free advertising on a couple of billboards along the highway. They advertised lodging and "Eat at World Famous Millie's Kitchen in the Picturesque Historic Town of Edenville." Never mind it being world famous, she remembered one time several German tourists made a special stop. They heard she was serving one of her German specialties, schnitzel and fried potatoes, with rolls and a little dish of sauerkraut to go along with it. She remembered their joyful praise, telling her how good it tasted, making them feel so welcome and at home. They each had a slice of her special apple pie with the lattice-work crust, brushed with a secret mixture, making it crunchy, buttery, and sweet. Millie had many secrets, and yearnings, too.

Impulsively, she decided to drive up to Walter Henry's place and pay his sister, Lulabelle, a visit. Last she heard, Walter Henry lived in an old miner's shack with his son, while Lulabelle, whom no one had seen in town for many years, lived nearby in a pretty little cabin. Flowers grew in window boxes Walter Henry built for her. A carved hand railing went up the steps and around the deck. Some of the older folks in town occasionally talked about Lulabelle, in reference to a tragic incident occurring over seventy years ago, though few truly cared, aside from Sam Goodman and Millie.

• • • •

Determined as she was, Millie was nervous, bracing herself, gripping the steering wheel tightly, and keeping her eyes on the steep dirt road ahead. Eventually, the so-called "miner's shack" came into view. It was a beautiful cabin, more like an A-framed Swiss chalet! In truth, what she saw was a newer cabin Walter Henry built, which hid the old miner's shack from view. Regardless of her mistake, she felt somewhat disgruntled. Pitying the three of them truly wasted her time, she thought. When the road swung sharply around to the right, the cabin was behind her. She drove through a stand of enormous pine trees with immense cones, many strewn about the ground beneath the trees. The road became bumpy. She nearly changed her mind, wondering what could have come over herself to attempt such a drive?

Grumbling and griping, she argued with her decision. She admitted she often closed the diner during the week for various reasons, but what thoroughly raised her ire, was to needlessly set out on a pleasure cruise into the mountains on a treacherous dirt road! She slowed her truck, bumping and rocking, the tires spinning and boulders tumbling. The road took another wide arc to her left, back toward Walter Henry's place, though higher up the mountainside, and this is when she saw the newest cabin that was Lulabelle's.

Millie was flabbergasted, awestruck, and even a bit mad. For years, she felt sorry for Lulabelle Henry, and here she was, living in the most beautiful place you ever did see, much nicer than her own home, Millie fumed. Pulling up to the cabin, she instantly felt awkward and embarrassed, hesitantly shutting off the engine and asking herself, "What am I doing here?" Her original reason, that she was out visiting "poor Lulabelle," was lost.

Millie spotted someone peering through a tiny window on the side of the cabin. She got out of the truck, bolstering her courage, and trying not to let her resentment show. The cabin door opened, and out stepped Lulabelle, a tiny, white-haired woman less than five-feet tall. Millie's heart rose in unexpected joy as though a ray of light shone upon her. Something about Lulabelle was a mysterious wonder. Millie's weak and silly resentment parted company with her strengthening and newly awakening heart. Stepping toward the front entrance, she noticed a small sign, a wooden plaque with words painted on it, reading: "Healing Waters Contemplation Center. All in need are welcome." She saw other women, sitting amongst the forest on benches or beside a manmade pool of water fed by a hot spring. Someone peacefully raked a pathway, bowers were being tended by another, trellised vines were snipped and clipped. Millie was delighted.

Lulabelle approached her, taking her hands in a welcoming clasp, gentle and soft. A peaceful smile showed unassuming kindness. Her wise eyes beheld Millie, who felt as a child, innocent, loved, and accepted. She and others had pitied Lulabelle, but it was they who were the pitiful ones, she learned.

Lulabelle greeted her, "Hello, Millie. I haven't seen you in years. I'm so glad you've come." She wore something like a coarse, homespun gunny sack. At closer view, Millie learned it was most likely a soft wool or cotton fabric, lightweight, simplicity itself, and *exquisite*, a word she never used prior to that moment.

"Well, Lulabelle, I don't know what to say," Millie began, feeling humbled and silly. "This is not what I expected."

"It's been a long time. And, please, call me 'Sister Ruth.' I've given my life to God and have forsaken who I was and everything the world expected of me. With the help of donations and the people who come to stay and work here, we've been able to create a place for spiritual seekers to find peace and reconnect with God's simple truths. Come." She took Millie's hand and guided her into the cabin and on a tour of the grounds. She showed her the other buildings, small cabins for guests, an outdoor chapel, and small amphitheater, everything surprising and remarkable in craftsmanship.

Millie repeated herself, "I'm sorry, Sister Ruth, but this is not what I had imagined." She explained, "Folks in Edenville talk about you from time to time. True, some have shared how beautiful it is up here, but most of us thought you had gone crazy and were living like a batty old hermit, or something. I'm sorry to say, I was among those who felt sorry for you, but… but…"

She stopped talking, as though something came over her. Having no idea what it was, Millie sensed she was being guided to surrender, to fully allow for what she was experiencing.

Sister Ruth, trained to be compassionate and to serve, understood the human condition and how spiritual practice could benefit a person like Millie. Born Lulabelle Henry, she was the first settler child born in the valley, over ninety years before. She smiled at her visitor. Light emanated from her face neither old nor young. "I've not thought about it for a long time. My life has become centered on God and how I may serve Him, to be His messenger, as well as His servant." A slight breeze drifted through the lofty forest trees, stirring the old woman's long, snowy-white wisp of hair.

Returning to the main cabin, Millie realized something about herself and confided in Sister Ruth, "Every place I ever went to work, every child I looked after and held in my arms," drawing her hands up to her heart, her lower lip quivering, "I just wanted to love everybody, I guess!" She glanced at Sister Ruth, then sat down on the cabin steps, adding, "I know now that I've been searching." She looked around her, into the trees, and noticed the magnificent view of their valley down below. Loose strands strayed from her pinned-up hair, lightly stirred by the cool air. More to herself, she said, "Maybe that's why I came here." She yearned to return to the world below, yet lacked the will to walk away from this new world she entered. She came there under false pretenses and now needed to speak the true reason for her visit.

"I see Walter and his son, Johnny," she finally confessed, "almost every day." She looked down at her hands that never knew a wedding ring, wrinkled, chapped, and red from washing dishes and wiping tables. "I used to think I loved Walter, that I'd want to marry him." She felt tears rising within her, still examining her aging hands, each finger, each bump and knobby joint. "And, oh! I *love* that boy!" Though she openly cried, she failed to understand. "Why?" She wanted to know and, imploring Sister Ruth, she repeated herself, "Why?"

At the sound of a truck approaching, Sister Ruth lightly touched Millie's shoulder, answering, "Maybe they can tell you."

Millie turned to see who was coming. She raised her hand to shade her eyes and saw it was Walter Henry and Johnny. Sister Ruth stepped off the porch to greet them. Before following her, Millie quickly dabbed her eyes with her handkerchief. To witness how they were in truth, not poor and deprived, but rich and at peace, had a quieting effect on her. How small the minds of those in town who dared to judge them! The stories and the gossip, the rumors by those who were truly poor, poor in spirit, proved themselves deprived, of truth and of beauty. Millie's heart resounded. She felt ashamed for believing these two menfolk needed her, all because of their scruffy hair and ripped clothing, the stains on their shirts and their skinny bodies. What could *she* possibly provide them? "How presumptuous," she chided herself. "How vain!"

"Hello, Millie. Hello, Sister." Walter Henry nodded his greeting to them, then reminded his son about his chores. "Why don't you show Millie the wood shop?"

Millie and Sister Ruth said their goodbyes. Millie promised, "I'll be back!"

Johnny took Millie's hand and led her to the old mining shack where his father made wooden decorative items, keepsakes, and useful items. He pointed out a variety of boxes, toothpick holders, plus some carved animals and toys. He told her they sold them at gift shops in the mountain resort areas.

Millie felt profoundly tired, more tired than she ever experienced. She was overwhelmed with goodness. What a wonderful life they led. She gave Johnny that hug she longed to give him. "I love you, Johnny. You're a good boy. Your father must be very proud of you." Giving him a quick kiss on the cheek, she thanked him for sharing the wood shop with her.

In a daze, she walked up the hillside toward her truck, to leave, as if a moment longer would render her incapable of leaving. She waved goodbye to Sister Ruth, standing on the porch beside her cabin, waving in return, and drove back to Edenville. Once she arrived at the diner, she saw Sam Goodman in front of his store, getting ready to close for the day. She told him she paid Lulabelle a visit.

Surprised, Sam asked, "You did? What'd she say?"

Instead of answering his question, Millie praised him. "You're a good man, Sam."

•　　•　　•

Walter Henry adopted Johnny more than ten years ago, after the boy was abandoned at the livery stable, like nothing more than an unwanted dog. The story they gave to anyone who asked, was that a cousin needed them to help out, saying she was unable to care for the boy. Most of the story was true. No one ever questioned it. The authorities never contacted them. Eventually, he and his sister legally adopted the child. They gave the boy the Henry name, raised him, loved him, and watched over and protected him. They were a family of sorts, but Walter Henry knew the boy needed a real family.

He never let it be known, but he also had feelings for the middle-aged owner of Millie's Kitchen, whom everyone, who knew her as long as he had, used to call, "Millie May." He had nothing to give her, was his excuse, and could not ask her to come and live as he did, in the rugged mountain forest. Years ago, he tried to put it out of his mind, though it never completely stayed away. After Millie left his house and his sister's retreat center, he was surprised how disappointed he felt. He missed her terribly, yet was pleased his son showed her the wood shop.

"Thank you, Johnny."

CHAPTER ELEVEN

Stepping onto his front porch, Jim Hart encountered the open door and, beyond, the disastrous state of his house. In shock, he paused momentarily to register the horrible scene. Tessie lay sprawled on the sofa, asleep, with the television blaring. Shep stood on a kitchen chair, his front paws on the table, lapping away at a bowl of unfinished cereal. Flies invaded every room, food lay out on the table, and stacks of dirty dishes covered the counter. Newspapers in shreds, unwashed laundry, and his hats and shoes strewn across the floor, struck him as an intentional display of his vengeful wife. Furious, he telephoned her at work. He was calm until she was put on the line.

"Beth?"

She said, "Yeah," and loudly sighed.

"What's the big idea leaving the place looking like a dump?"

"What's the big idea being gone all night?!"

"I fell asleep at work. It was a mistake. The dog's are in here. They made a mess. There's flies, cuz you left the door open. Man! The-the-the-whole place is smelly, too!"

"Why don't you have Little Miss Sylvia come over and clean it for you!! She's more your wife than I am, you—"

A co-worker grabbed the phone away from Beth and, before hanging up, informed Jim, "This phone is not to be used for personal calls!"

Jim studied the mess in the kitchen, his wife's resentment clearly expressed in opened jars of sticky grape jelly and peanut butter and in dry bread and stale potato chips. A trapped fly helplessly buzzing within an empty doughnut box motivated him to act. He attempted to clean what years of neglect and his wife's bitterness inflicted upon their home. It only served to threaten his one remaining vestige of hope. Giving up, he got ready for work, then walked the path to the blacksmith shop and livery stable, so far the only normal part of his day. Once he saw Walter Henry, he hesitated at the doorway of the barn, immediately spotting the empty whiskey bottle on the ground by the stool. His hope faltered. That old, sorrowful shame he knew well, slowly bore its way into his heart, and the goodness that strived to rise during one brief walk to work, sunk into his gut.

Together, he and his partner fed the horses in silence, brushed them, and checked their wounds where the vet had removed some bandages. At their owner's home, they kicked down the corral fence when a fire started in a shed near the house. They ran loose in a state of panic and got injured. One horse, Siam, was a beautiful buckskin mare. The other horse, Bossy, was a fat one who loved to eat. A bit swayback, she bore a brilliant chestnut coat and glistening flaxen mane and tail. Though they belonged to a teenaged girl who lived nearby, Jim loved the two horses as if they were his own. Tending to them, his mood softened when Siam turned her head to gently nudge his own when he stood near. He caught his tears before they had a chance to run. One worried glance at Walter Henry looking his way, told Jim they were there all the same.

After they got the horse trailer hitched onto Jim's truck and loaded the horses, Walter Henry announced he would stay and clean the stalls and the corral, even though they usually shared in the task. Feeling guilty, Jim took the horses home. Their owners paid him a little extra, praising Jim on how nice they looked. Though, all Jim remembered when he drove away, was the softness of the mare's shiny coat beneath his touch as he said goodbye.

Back at the livery stable, Jim unhitched the horse trailer and traded it for the farrier's rig. He thought about how much his partner tolerated, always supportive, too. Before getting into his truck, he humbly thanked Walter Henry, hoping the old man understood.

Once Jim rounded the corner and disappeared from sight, Walter Henry placed his hands on his hips and looked down at the ground. His memory appeared within the dusty tracks of horse's hooves and boot heels. When two of the newspapermen next door brought chairs out to sit and eat their lunch, the old blacksmith retreated into the barn.

• • •

An important client in the valley was Jim's next destination. He wanted to make a good impression, so he dressed in his best jeans and combed his hair extra neat. It paid off, because they offered him a job as an assistant to their resident farrier.

The manager spoke with Jim before he left. "We need you here full time," he said. "This is a big operation and we want only the finest care for our horses." He patted the young man on the back as Jim got ready to leave. "Talk it over with your wife and let us know right away. Hope you'll do it!"

Jim was ecstatic and felt a boost of confidence breaking through the shadows he struggled to hold at bay. He replied instantly, "Thank you, Mr. Reynolds! I want the job! I'm ready for it!"

"I'm sure you are."

When Jim sat in his truck and closed the door, Mr. Reynolds stepped closer and patted him on the shoulder. "Your dad meant the world to us, Jim. We want to do right by him and give his son first consideration." He smiled and added, "We kinda like you, too, just between the two of us."

Jim smiled back at the man like the sun could actually penetrate his darkening soul. He felt like a boy again, with a father who was proud of him. He said, "Thank you," and left for home.

Tired and dirty, he parked his rig alongside the blacksmith shop and walked to his house. He gave a somber hello to Beth, noticing there was no dinner and nothing had been cleaned further than he had done that morning. She slipped into the bathroom and stayed there so long, he was unable to get a bath. Frustrated, he washed the dishes, scrubbed the kitchen table, pushed in the chairs, and began sweeping the floor, but could no longer stand the sight of the place.

He telephoned Sylvia, using their code words for where to meet, although he told Beth he was going to a friend's house. "Probably be gone until late," he said. He put a change of clothes in a sack, changed his shoes, then walked a short way up the driveway before taking a quick detour. In the deep shade of some densely growing pines, he waited for Sylvia. Hearing some footsteps, he hurried to greet her, feeling both relieved and desperate.

Together, they fled into the enveloping night. They were young lovers again, all was good, and they were free. They got a room at their local Nighty-Nite Lucky 7 Motel by the highway, ate pizza, and laughed out loud. Later, as they lay facing each other on the bed, Jim recalled the job offer he received earlier that day, and asked, "Would you leave your husband for me?" He waited and saw her hesitate and roll her eyes in evasion, smiling weakly, before he put the question to her again, "Sylvia, answer me! Would you leave your husband for me?"

She answered as she drew away from him, "I don't know. I don't know if I could do that," which was the truth.

It shocked Jim and he grew angry. "What do you mean, you don't know?! You love me, don't you?!"

Sylvia hushed him. "Don't be mad." She explained she was merely surprised by the question.

Underneath the weak apology Jim gave her, the door to his inner darkness crept open. Sliding closer to her, he kissed her, holding her arm in his grip, tight and firm.

Sylvia's heart raced in terror and she tried to pull away. "You're hurting me," she cried, stunned at the change in him.

He jerked her toward him. "You're *mine!* You got that?!"

She froze and began to cry.

Nevertheless, he continued, "If I say you're coming with me, you're coming with me. All right?" He kissed her again, but Sylvia turned her head away. Disgusted with himself, he got up off the bed and dressed. After hastily stuffing the rest of his things in the grocery sack, he left the room. Getting a drink was the only thing on his mind now, and she—

Hating him, Sylvia rushed to shower, got dressed, and grabbed her purse. At first, when she left the motel, she began walking home, but quickly changed direction. Despite Jim's coarseness, he awakened in her the real possibility of leaving her husband. She thought of someone she could turn to for help. Darting through the shadows, she tried to hide from people out late at night. Car lights shone upon her, frightening her. She wavered, no longer certain which direction to take.

Deciding to go home, she struggled with her fear, when someone grabbed her from out of the darkness. Beginning to scream, the unknown arms and hands on her became Jim's. It was Jim, gently pulling her into his embrace, saying how sorry he was, while she cried in his arms and he swore it would never happen again. Sylvia believed him and let him escort her back to their motel room where they consummated the vows they both made. He would never harm her again and she would leave her husband. However, Jim would break his vow, while Sylvia would keep her's.

CHAPTER TWELVE

Forty anxiously awaited Sylvia's return, pacing the floor of his barren living room late into the night. Throw rugs occasionally dampened the clomping of his shoes upon the scuffed wood floor. He held his Bible in one hand and an old derringer in the other, a lucky find from the rubble of his neighbor's burned house. Even though it lacked bullets, he felt its power in his grip.

The dark room which held him, boasted a drab, olive green sofa, a scratched coffee table with ashtray, and a standing lamp. The fringe-bedecked lampshade caught his attention, appalled to see it draped in dust and laced with cobwebs. The wood flooring, he now admitted, was minimally cleaned. No curtains adorned the front window, no pictures or hangings of any kind graced the walls. What used to impress him as his wife's thriftiness, now dawned on him as her lack of interest in their home.

Forty wondered why Sylvia never asked to take a vacation, which then reminded him of his family. The few trips they took were before his teenaged sister ran away from home. His parents hired a detective, who discovered she had married a boy, got pregnant, and then died while giving birth. He never forgot the day the hired investigator talked with his parents. Watching the tall man in his nice gray suit, gray fedora angled a particular way, left Forty in awe. His fervent wish to be a detective was born in that moment. First, his brother died from polio, when only a small child. His mother devoted herself to her two remaining children, while his father, foreman of the fruit pickers and migrant farm laborers in Edenville, gave himself to his work. Once Forty's sister died, he feared losing their few remaining family members. Only now did he realize that he blamed his sister for the way his father treated his mother.

His parents buried his brother at the county cemetery, because his father would not allow the boy to be buried in the Catholic burial ground. The child's personal items were interred in their backyard by his mother, tokens holding special memories for her, she told Forty. Apparently, it helped her to cope with loss as she added her daughter's mementos to the eerie memorial. It grew over time into a sanctuary, of sorts, as Forty's father became increasingly abusive and as they grew apart. Flowering plants flourished, decorative items twirled in the wind and spun around, and there were bird feeders and bird baths in her garden. Little stones she found while meandering across the fields and through the woods around town, were placed in selected locations.

Forty's mother wandered further afield until, one day, she failed to return. People reported sightings of her, some far-fetched and too-far-afield, but there was one authenticated report of her seen hitchhiking on the coast highway with some hippies. Someone from Edenville investigated her absence. They wrote for *The Edenville Weekly* and wanted to do a story, a human interest piece with pictures included. One of those pictures was, unmistakably, of Forty's mother. He paid big money to the journalist not to run the story. The photographs, which he kept, served as a potent reminder of what went wrong with his family.

His father nastily proclaimed every opinion he held, often ranting loudly, "She was no good from the start! It's all her fault!" Forty helped him discard his mother's possessions neither of them wanted. His father ordered him to "haul it all to the dump where it belongs!" His mother's Bible, Forty now clutched in his zealous grip. She was a devout Catholic, a religion his father criticized harshly, cigar held between his fingers. "Nuthin' but a bunch of damned profligates! Corrupt to their papal core! They'd be better off sinning out in the open like the rest of us heathens!" Forty feared his father, recalling this particular outburst, his father's armpits sweating heavily through his worn-out, army green t-shirt. The wetness had become ringed with salt and with grime.

Forty did the same for Sylvia's father, out of a sense of husbandly duty, though now he believed it was what the Lord called him to do. Acting as Jesus' private eye, he took it upon himself to scour each home for clues to, first, his mother's wayward end and, second, his wife's erring ways. Searching through Ev Mendoza's burned house, he hoped to find any clues connected to her housekeeper. He first saw the young man from the fire crew with her, riding in her car, going toward Ev's. Forty Sumner truly believed an investigative nature was his cross to bear. He bore it with courage and with fortitude.

"That's me!" He shouted proudly to the darkened house, "Forty! For-ti-tude!"

Emboldened by this play on words, he thrust the Bible out before him, high aloft. Unexpectedly, the truth bore down upon him until he could bear its weight no more. He fled the scene to search for his wife and the man responsible for her going astray.

First, he consulted with another authority, *Detective's Digest Special Crime Investigator's Edition for Collectors*, full of gadgets, everything for the crime buff. He read an article that held special meaning for him, so he ran upstairs where he stored past issues in boxes. It was a true-life account regarding a crime solved in the city of Fanning Beltway. Even Forty's exceptionally unbounded imagination could not grasp the unusual name. Shaking his head, he said, "Shoo-wee! That's nuts!" He read aloud what he underlined in red ink, "Fanning Beltway citizens are breathing a big sigh of relief as private investigators zero in on a rash of bank robberies carried out by the notorious—" Forty scanned the article, until he found what he was looking for, then went on, "One private investigator, hired by a local bank that would not release any details other than his name, Pierson Adleberry, is credited with connecting evidence left at their bank to one of the robbers, who was a janitor for all the banks robbed."

Forty repeated the name, "Pierson Adleberry," with a faraway look in his eyes. He whistled between his front teeth and lower lip, the way his father did while reading his own magazines.

Forty's father kept his magazine collection in boxes in a shed by the fruit packing warehouse. He instructed his son never to go in there, but Forty spied on his father often, especially during the long summer months when he and his friends grew bored. Forty recalled one day in particular, when they peered in the murky and aged shed window. Tucker went first, standing on an apple crate and peeking in the window. He hurriedly jumped down and said, "Let's go do something else!" He took Sylvia's hand and began to leave. Forty rushed to take his turn, grabbing the window sill and pulling himself up onto the wobbly crate. Only a blurred image of his father could be seen, turning his magazine another direction and unfolding the page. Nevertheless, Forty saw and heard his father whistle, striving to imitate him ever since.

Not wanting to dwell on the past, he tossed the magazine aside and left his house. He started to head down the alleyway toward Tucker Stewart's house, but hesitated, considering his initial suspicion regarding Jim Hart. Conflicted over what to do, he thought of Pierson Adleberry. To solve the case, Adleberry carried out a thorough investigation, questioning everyone involved, working tirelessly toward success. Recalling the words of Sylvia's Aunt Justice, "You are the Lord's private eye, Fortuitous," he decided to go to Jim Hart's house.

From the main dirt road, he hurried toward the Hart's driveway, which led through a grove of pine trees that made the night appear darker. Finding it difficult to see, he stopped. Shep and Tessie were barking. He forgot about the dogs, imagining them coming after— Oh no! Someone else was out in the night! Forty heard them running recklessly up the driveway. The moment he recognized who it was, they collided into him, knocking him to the ground, unconscious.

Beth turned on her porch light and hung out the front doorway, eyes squinting. With a vituperative scowl on her face, she yelled at the dogs to "get back here!" Her bitter voice had a growl in it, due to the lack of sweetness or niceties in herself of late. She had plans of her own and let the dogs go, like she had the house.

The next morning, while on her way to work, she encountered Forty sitting on her driveway, looking dazed and rubbing the back of his head and his shoulder. She stopped the car and, leaving the engine running, rushed to his side. "Forty!" She knelt down, put her hand on his back, and questioned him. "What happened to you?! What are you doing here?!"

"I-I'm not sure." He shook his head as if to rattle his senses back and, panicking, began hopping and scooting around where he sat, nearly blurting out, "My gun!" Fortunately, he caught himself and instead proclaimed, "Someone was in your driveway! They must have knocked me out," which was absolutely true.

"What?!" Beth thought it might have been her husband, but—

"I think it was someone—" He vaguely remembered the young man on the fire crew. He tried standing, but almost fainted.

Beth grabbed him. "Here, let me take you over to Spring Hill. I was just going to work." She aided Forty into the passenger side of the car. After closing the car door and walking around to the driver's side, she spotted the small gun and the Bible laying beside the driveway. She picked them up and, once seated in the car, started giving them to Forty, but drew them toward herself with a look of concern on her face. "Are these yours?"

He took the Bible, politely answering, "Just this."

At the rest home, a nurse examined Forty, advising him to lie down while she arranged to drive him home. Soon afterward, they left the rest home, passing Beth's car in the parking area. Forty made up an excuse, telling the nurse he left something in it. Retrieving the gun, he stuffed it down the back of his pant's waistline, something he always wanted to do. Rejoining the nurse, he lied to her. "It's not there," he said.

Meanwhile, Beth was sitting on a tall stool at a counter while flipping through a magazine on her break, drinking a cup of strong coffee, and eating a jelly-filled doughnut from a pink box. She wondered what happened at her house last night. She knew young people were always sneaking around late at night and figured Forty—

"Wait a minute!" It dawned on her that "Forty must have thought his wife was at *our house—with my husband!*" She shrieked, "*Oh, sh—!*" If that was what Forty thought, she deduced, "*Then, he knows, too!*" She began to panic. Slamming the heel of her hand onto her forehead, she exclaimed, "What a *dope* I am!" She ran out to the car to get the gun, but it was gone! She thought Forty must have been planning to shoot— "No! It must have belonged to whoever knocked him down!" That made more sense to her and she became horrified. "If that other person had the gun—" She began to fear they may have been on their way to— "No. That's ridiculous!"

She told her co-workers what took place. They let her use the phone this time, so she could call the sheriff. Deputy Bob Carson soon arrived at the rest home to get her story. She told him *everything*, including her suspicions about her husband having an affair with the wife of the man she found in her driveway. "Little Miss Sylvia *Cutsie*-Pie," she derisively muttered to herself. The deputy thanked her and left.

On his way to Forty's house, he passed the nurse on her return trip to the rest home. Once he arrived, the deputy grilled Forty about the gun. Forty denied it being his or even having it, suggesting, "The criminal may have retrieved it from Mrs. Hart's car." He was Pierson Adleberry once more, wanting to solve this case without that "meddling, incompetent deputy," as he often remarked about the man.

"C'mon, Forty, you can tell me."

Bob talked Forty into admitting, "Yes, I was out looking for my wife. She went to visit a neighbor friend. I grew worried and went over to get her, so she wouldn't have to walk home alone in the dark." He stood firm by his story.

The deputy believed nary a word. He knew Beth Hart well enough to know she was no liar, but had nothing on her husband fooling around with Forty's wife, other than suspicious sightings and gossip. Reluctantly, he said, "All right, Forty," smacking him on the leg and shaking it around a bit, as a goodbye to a good ole buddy. "I'm gonna give you this one." Starting to walk outside, he rubbed his face, smoothed his beard with his hand, placed his hands on his hips where his gun belt rested, and sadly concluded, "Seeing as how the only one hurt around here is you."

Stalling, he paused after going down each step of the porch, pounding a fist lightly on the banister. He surveyed the Sumner's porch and yard. "Man, what a sad-looking place."

Forty followed the deputy outside. "I-I better go lay down, Officer. And I need to call into work, too."

Deputy Carson swung around, realizing Forty was merely a victim of his wife's troubles everyone talked about, yet no one could prove. "Okay, Forty," he said. You get some rest."

CHAPTER THIRTEEN

Autumn passed, followed by a cold, wet winter. The residents of Edenville and Pine Way rejoiced when the days finally warmed in spring. Elm trees began leafing out along with maple and oak. Wildflowers bloomed in grand displays of pink and yellow, purple and white, expansive splashes of color painted across the green backdrop of grassy hillsides. Their scent, sweet and heady, perfumed the air, drawing many into field and forest to picnic or to stroll. Large ponds and puddles filled the low-lying areas where ducks dabbled and raised their young.

Candelaria sat on her porch steps writing in her new notebook. She filled the first one with poems, stories, and memories, which is what she recorded on this day.

"Listen to me, children," her grandmother said. "Don't ever be ashamed to be Mexican." Her grandmother led them into the woods for this story, on a day similar to the one Candelaria now enjoyed. The fragrant aroma of flowers, like millions of tiny roses, drifted to her from the apple orchards as she gradually stepped further into the past. Her grandmother pointed out to them whatever caught her interest, maybe a plant or two, or an insect, telling them something important about each discovery. Her brothers were more interested in trying to hit tree trunks with rocks or catching lizards. Candelaria and her sister, Gilda, short for Hermenegilda, loved those woodland jaunts.

Her grandmother, Mama Stefa, continued, as they walked along, "To be Mexican is to be a passionate person, a lover of life, of food, and of family. We love to sing and dance." She held her hands in the air as though taking her imaginary partner's hands into her own. Candelaria and Gilda looked at one another, trying not to giggle as their grandmother held up the edge of her skirt and danced around, imaginary music filling the air for her and her partner. Gilda tried to get Candelaria to laugh, crossing her eyes with hands raised in the air, which worked. Candelaria was a little girl in pigtails then and loved to have fun. Mama Stefa grabbed Gilda and held her giggling, squirming body, hugging and kissing her before she ran off to join her brothers.

After one such storytelling venture, her grandmother held up her index finger, imparting this important lesson, "To say you are 'Mexican,' means you are a person from Mexico, or of the people of Mexico, and that is *your* heritage." Turning her head side to side, she lovingly advised, "Never forget that." Mama Stefa ended her lesson with, "I am not from Mexico. I was born in the United States. Mexico is in my blood, in my ancestry, like it is for the four of you."

When the story ended, Candelaria and her siblings gathered around their grandmother, wanting to see what she brought for their picnic. Candelaria could still hear their voices, like a beautiful, faraway song. Its sweetness, as cherished as the fragrance of flowers drifting on the spring breeze, nurtured her heart.

Candelaria loved the memory, but her grandmother's belief about what it meant to be Mexican, was a poor fit for her. She wanted to be herself. Why was it so hard for her to find? Considering the way others treated her as a child, and that she preferred the company of other Mexicans, she understood. To take it one step further, connecting herself to Mexico, a distant place, she found impossible to accept. Nevertheless, she longed to embrace her people, her Mexican-American-ness, and to carry it proudly in her heart.

Exasperated with this quest of her's, Candelaria closed the notebook, needing to do something more. The school's librarian, Miss Winters, promised her she could use the typewriter in her office after school. Candelaria thought someone might want to publish what she wrote. Leaving the house, she took a shortcut through the woods, going in the direction of the school. Walking along the path, she thought about her son. Since her mother's funeral, months ago, she avoided him. Everything within herself was changing, deepening, opening her to something new. She felt much too vulnerable to approach him now. At the church, she detected an angry bitterness in his demeanor. Rosa mentioned the drastic change in her brother. Yet, Candelaria strived to love her son, noting his strength while standing alongside the other men. She felt proud of him.

To her surprise, her brothers attended their mother's funeral. "At least they did that much," she commented to herself. She gave her mother a full Mass and several of her friends and one of her brothers read passages from the Bible. The entire day was very hard for her, but, miraculously, it turned out fine. The work and the waiting was over. Since then, she adjusted to life without another family member with whom to share it. If this thought did not make her feel old enough, helping her daughter, Rosa, prepare for her wedding certainly did. Nevertheless, she was happy, content, and praying for lots of grandchildren.

She thought again about her son and knew something very troublesome was on his mind. How she wanted to talk to him like when he was a boy, but he had a wife. Beth's absence at the funeral hurt her more than the lack of invitations to their house. What was she like now? She wondered, so she sought an answer from Rosa. Her daughter made a look, meaning, "Don't ask!" Rosa's eyes rolled and she tightened her face as though straining to keep herself from saying something unpleasant. Buster attended and even sat with them. It was a good sign. He took her hand as she and Rosa walked to the front pew in church. Candelaria was pleased and knew Rosa would do fine as his wife. He got promoted at the hardware store and planned to become an assistant manager to the owner, himself, Mr. Goodman. She also inquired about Jim, but Rosa turned her head the other way and, excusing herself, left Candelaria's side to talk to someone else.

Candelaria's closest friend, Esther, told her, "Stop worrying." They spoke privately at the gathering after Mass. Esther said, "Men don't talk about things, especially to their mothers." She seemed determined to impress upon Candelaria it was best to let it go, challenging her, "What kind of man would he be if he talked things over with his mother?"

Defiantly and righteously, Candelaria said aloud to the sky, "A *good* man! That's what kind of man he would be!" She knew it was true. He was keeping a secret that was destroying him, causing harm to every person who knew him. This awareness came as a shock to Candelaria who was unprepared for such violent truth. It shook her to her very soul. "Dear God!" She quickly veered off the path to sit in the woods, and cried, "My boy! My son!" Sitting on the grass sobbing, she knew she needed to take action of some kind. For now, she could only think to get up off the damp ground and continue walking toward the school.

It looked deserted, except for the janitor and a few employees and students staying after school. Slipping into a restroom, she took time to compose herself, wash her face, and calm down. In the librarian's office, she struggled to do some typing, but could only think of her son. Months had passed since she saw him last. Could he be worse now? She stopped those thoughts, thinking instead about her mother and her grandmother, which brought her peace of mind, enabling her to return to her typing. After an hour or two, the librarian announced it was time to close up for the day and go home. Candelaria thanked her and was welcomed to come any day after school. She appreciated Miss Winters, always friendly.

"Why couldn't my son have married someone like her?" she pondered, and left the library to go home.

On her way, she walked to the rectory across from the church. The priest's housekeeper let her in and led her to a quiet, yet stuffy office. Soon, Father Sanchez breezed in and took her hand.

"Hello, Laria!"

His deep, sonorous voice always caught her off guard.

"So good to see you!"

Father Sanchez was the new priest who replaced Father Jovial, who had retired.

Candelaria felt uncomfortable at first, remembering another thought she once had. His voice was like those of the most attractive leading men in the old, black-and-white movies she and her husband once enjoyed together. She told herself, "It's just advice," and to stop those silly thoughts. Checking her reaction again, she reminded herself that Father Sanchez was a younger man, and a priest, for heaven's sake!

"I wondered if I could seek your advice, Father. It's about my son." She felt relieved, having taken the first step.

"What can I help you with?"

"My—my son, Jim, he—" Candelaria became aware she based her concerns solely on intuition. Nevertheless, she continued, "He looks troubled, Father. I don't know what to do, to ask him about it or to let it go." The priest listened carefully to her, seated in an upholstered chair opposite from where she sat. She thought he was so handsome, and tried to picture him in his vestments, which helped, then finished her entreaty, "People have been telling me not to worry, but how can I not worry? I'm his mother!" Her careworn face revealed the strain under which she dwelt.

The priest whole-heartedly believed that worry undermined faith. He knew Candelaria to be a woman who lived for her family, who served God through serving her family. Yet, in a brief lapse of faith, himself, he judged such a woman knew not how to listen directly to God nor how to trust in Him. Emotional and sensitive, he further believed, she listened to signs, to a breath of wind, or the scent of roses. This woman who sat before him, reminded him of his own mother, who also worried needlessly.

"My dear." Father Sanchez paused momentarily before telling her the story of his own troubled youth. It was not a long story, but he was sure to add what he knew about her son, personally, without breaking a confidence. "Jim is a very proud man. He must work things out on his own, even if he fails. He is trying so hard to make his family proud of him, but doesn't know how to talk about it. This is typical of a lot of men. It's your son's way, part of the way he is, the way God made him."

His tone softened and he spoke more tenderly, enrapturing Candelaria's attention. "We all struggle, Laria. It's the workload God gives to us. It's how He teaches us, tests us. It's how we learn to rely on Him and to love Him, no matter what." He told Candelaria exactly what he wished someone had told his mother those days long ago.

Unfortunately, Candelaria only heard, "no matter what." Snapping out of her momentary daze, she cried, "But, Father! I'm afraid he's going to—" She stopped. She could not bear to walk this road any further. Something prevented her. It took her breath away, like a hand pressing down on her chest. She froze in complete understanding. If her son destroyed himself, he would destroy anyone who got too close to whatever tortured him so relentlessly.

"Let's pray. Okay?"

She agreed to listen to and accompany Father Sanchez.

He prayed for peace and healing to enter Jim's heart, that he would open to receive God's love and guidance. He asked God to bring peace to Candelaria, to help her to let her son fight his battles as a man. Lastly, he took her hands and clasped them in his own. "Take care, Laria." He smiled and laughed lightly. "We live in such drama, in such—heartache and suffering. Why don't you let God carry this one? Hmm?"

He was younger than Candelaria, though wise, she thought. Difficult as it was, she knew he was right. She could not carry Jim anymore. She resolved to let him go, "no matter what."

CHAPTER FOURTEEN

During lunch, Rosa left work and drove to Pine Way. She had her own concerns for her brother and her own methods of reaching out to him. Parking at the blacksmith shop, she spotted Walter Henry shoeing a horse. Heedless of the man's occupation at the moment, she interrupted him.

"Is Jim around?"

He glanced awkwardly her way, his mouth holding horseshoe nails, then returned to hammering a shoe in place. Not wanting to wait for him, she walked back to her car. She retrieved Jim's football medal from the glove box and tucked it into a special lunch she packed for him. Hoping to brighten his day, and maybe get him talking, she set the paper sack on the workbench and left.

Once he finished his task, Walter Henry stopped to take a peek at what was in the lunch bag. He was famished. Jim was working elsewhere that day and would certainly not want the food to go to waste. He drew out a sandwich and began eating. When it was time to pick up Johnny from school, he handed him the lunch and said, "Here! You can have what's left."

With relish, the boy reached in, grabbed a sandwich and ate it as they drove up the hill to their cabin. Once there, he carried it into the house, dug through it, and happily discovered some cookies, plus something else. From the bottom of the sack, Johnny drew Jim's medal into view. His eyes grew wide in amazement. Hurrying off to his room, though chores and homework awaited him, he pulled a shoebox from its hiding place beneath his bed. Carefully lifting the lid, he withdrew the leather scrapbook. It had the words, "Grandma's Little Brag Book," embossed on its soft, velvet-like cover. The letters had been dyed red and, in one corner, two green leaves held a single, yellow rose.

Walter Henry called to him, "Johnny! Time to get to your chores, son!"

Flipping through the pages, Johnny discovered the album contained pictures of Jim Hart. On the last page was a picture of Jim in his graduation gown, the very same medal around his neck, which Johnny now held in his hand. He was in awe.

Again, his father shouted, "Johnny! What'd I tell you?!"

Footsteps began approaching the room. Johnny frantically hid everything and got up to leave right away. His heart overflowed with excitement.

Tending to his chores, he swept the floor, took the trash out to the incinerator to burn, chopped kindling wood and, along with a few split logs, stacked it by the fireplace. He swept shavings off the floor of the wood shop and dumped them in a pile outside. Each chore was addressed absentmindedly, because his thoughts were consumed with his latest find, Jim Hart's medal. It now lay amongst other treasures, like a necklace he pretended belonged to his real mother and, of course, the scrapbook.

Everyone had a mother and father. Johnny knew Walter Henry and Lulabelle were not his parents. They were brother and sister. He heard the comments going around town and at school over the years. "Whose boy is that child, anyway? I know! I bet he's—" What really turned his head was when someone said, "Just look at him. He's the exact image!"

Needing to know the truth, he searched and searched and, one day, found proof. Amongst Walter Henry's important papers, he discovered his adoption papers. Ever since he found them, he secretly wished and fervently hoped that Jim Hart was his real father. Johnny never forgot the time Jim picked him up and held him in his arms, hugging him. The love Johnny felt in that embrace was fading, but it was not forgotten. Only two people in the whole world held this special place. One of them, was Jim. The other, well, he had a hunch, but he was unsure. Once, he saw a woman driving by the school, several years ago, a stranger with short, reddish blond hair. She was looking at him intently. It frightened him. He never forgot it, but also wondered if she might be his mother. He thought of her when he held the necklace in his hand. A small silver crucifix on a silver chain, it held a tiny, green stone at its center, his mother's birthstone, he pretended. Every so often, he dreamed of days far gone and could remember a woman at a house...but it was fleeting. Johnny's life's wish, to be reunited with his real mother and father, now seemed possible. While pretending gave him hope, these two people he carried in his heart gave him a dream.

• • •

When Esther Gutierrez and her husband arrived home from work that afternoon, she looked over at Candelaria's, wondering what happened to her. Her friend missed work and the farmworkers' meeting afterward. Deciding to check on her neighbor, Esther learned that Candelaria was ill. Before she pitched in to help take care of her, though, she called Rosa at work to let her know. Rosa came home right away. Together, they devised a way to care for her mother. Candelaria, in no position to argue, tried to stop them.

"Hey! I'm half Indian. Being Indian means I know how to take care of myself!"

"I see you've been doing just fine," chimed in her neighbor, being Chavie. "It's all over your feverish face and messy kitchen!"

Rosa confided in Esther. "I don't know what's gotten into her."

Concerned, Esther looked at her while wiping the kitchen counter down, saying, "What do you mean?"

"I can hear you two," came a weak voice from the bedroom. "Might as well talk normal."

Esther-Chavie walked back to the bedroom before saying, "You behave yourself and rest, you hear me?"

Candelaria moaned. "I can't believe this."

"Eh?!"

"All right! All right!" Candelaria finally agreed.

Esther returned to the kitchen and jerked her head in the direction of the front door, signaling Rosa to follow her outside. The whole area where they lived sat beneath the woodland's shade the entire day, but, as the sun lowered behind the ridge, the shade grew darker and the colors in the sky deepened. Golden rays of sunlight burst between the branches of the trees. Their clothing and everything around them shone in hues from the evening's golden light.

"Tell me," Esther asked Rosa, "what's been happening?" She worried, because she heard occasional comments from Candelaria.

Rosa shared similar comments.

Candelaria tried to shout, "I know you're out there talking about me! Indians have super hearing!"

Esther and Rosa laughed out loud. Dismissing it, they talked quietly between themselves. Esther held a dish towel in her hand, swinging it through the air as she expressed herself, her arms going out this way and that. She told Rosa what she knew about Rosa's ancestry. She knew about Candelaria's grandparents, her father's parents. She said Ev and Jesse Mendoza, Candelaria's parents, always had a big vegetable garden. Esther's family, at one time, had very little to eat. Jesse came to their camp, at a time when the migrant farmworkers lived in tents. He brought lettuce, peppers, corn, and even some strawberries. He was like an angel to them. Her family was new to the area, competing with other hungry families for work. Her father thanked Jesse and invited him to sit awhile. On upended logs of wood, they sat together by the campfire, talking about the old days.

Rosa listened to Esther relate the story. She stood rapt with attention, as if she had been hungry and this woman gave her the food for which she hungered.

Esther continued, "I heard them talking about Mexico, the Revolution, and Pancho Villa. My father saw him once in Juarez. That's why so many people left Mexico, you know?"

Rosa was dumbfounded. She never heard anything about having any connection to the actual country. "Mexico? Revolution?!"

"Sí, mi hermana." Esther referred to Rosa as her 'hermana,' her sister, out of national pride and their shared Mexican heritage.

Rosa was near tears, her youthful face one of inspiration and love. "No one ever told me about this."

Esther went on to say, she specifically heard Rosa's grandfather mention that his mother was not Mexican. She was a full-blooded Indian from a local tribe once living in their area. "That means, your great-great—"

"You mean I'm Indian, too?"

Esther took a pose, one hand on a hip, looking dumbfounded at Rosa. "Don't you know anything about where babies come from?" She turned on her heels, pretending to walk away from this silly young woman, then turned back around to criticize Rosa. "And, you're getting married?!"

Rosa laughed at Esther. "Of course, I do! Why do you *think* we're getting married?" Her hand shot up to her mouth to cover it, knowing she said too much to the wrong person.

Esther looked at her with a serious face and brought the palms of her hands up to the sides of her head to cover her ears. "I'm gonna pretend I didn't hear that!" She took them down and, feeling more and more like Chavie, wagged her finger through the air as a warning to Rosa. "But, if I ever hear so much as a *peep* about you and Buster doing you-know-what—" She made a line with her finger across her neck.

"What?!" Rosa was shouting. "You wouldn't do that!"

"No, you're right." Esther-Chavie leaned toward Rosa and stated very clearly, "I would do it to Buster. Only, I would do it in a place, so he could no longer do 'it' anymore." Pleased with herself, she sashayed proudly up the steps of the porch and into the house.

Rosa knew Esther was only playacting, but decided it was a good idea to curtail her secret meetings with Buster. Taking a deep breath in and blowing it out with gusto, she prepared herself for the occasion. "Well, Buster, you're gonna have to learn a new word, and it's not going to be 'yes' anymore, until our wedding night."

Half-heartedly planning to tell Buster the new rules, she joined Esther in putting together a tray for her mother's dinner. They heated a can of chicken noodle soup, placed soda crackers beside her bowl, along with a few slices of orange, and a cup of water.

When Esther brought the tray into Candelaria's room, Candelaria pretended to be sound asleep. She heard Rosa's accidental admission and wanted to forget what she heard. She silently prayed the children would not come until a year after the wedding.

"Laria." Esther nudged Candelaria, who pretended to awaken. Esther laughed. "Look who's faking. I bet you heard everything, didn't you?"

Candelaria ignored Esther. To Rosa, on the other hand, before going to sleep that night, she warned her in private. "No babies until you're married for a year! Promise me, Rosa."

Rosa promised, as much as she regretted being a loud mouth. Not only Buster, but she, too, would have to learn, 'no.'

"Hey!" Candelaria raised her index finger, declaring the law. "I heard what Chavie said, and that goes for me, too."

Rosa challenged her mother playfully, "What's with the finger already? When did you get to be so, so *macho?*" She left the bedroom and, returning to her previous thoughts about her and Buster, she got herself ready for bed, only partially listening to her mother's reply.

"When I stood on the steps of the state capitol and saw my shadow, my darling daughter."

CHAPTER FIFTEEN

Candelaria stood in the small, sunlit office, gathering her papers and preparing to go home. Quiet conversation between herself and the librarian, centered around her latest story.

"You ought to send it to a magazine, Larie," Miss Winters suggested. "Or, maybe a newspaper might print it."

Walter Henry entered the library with his son, interrupting their discussion. Candelaria noticed Miss Winters instantly come to life, cheerfully calling to the boy, "Johnny! Come on in here!" Johnny stepped into her office, wearing Jim's medal.

Candelaria demanded, "Where did you get that medal?!"

Clutching it tightly in his hand, Johnny bowed his head and timidly answered, "Jim gave it to me. He says I'm his hero."

Walter Henry placed his hand on the boy's shoulder during this tense encounter with Jim's mother. Although, what he noticed more than anything, was Miss Winters, her mood turning serious as she strangely eyed the prize encircling Johnny's neck. He thought she looked vaguely familiar and wondered what was going on, when Candelaria suddenly excused herself, almost fleeing the room in a huff. He decided it was best to ignore it and tend to the reason for their visit.

"Umm...Johnny needs his own library card. I seem to have lost mine."

Once Miss Winters was busy helping Johnny, Walter Henry slowly edged his way out the door, hoping Jim's mother was long gone. Considering the strange encounter with the two ladies, he deemed it wise to sit in the truck and wait. Unfortunately, he gave little thought as to how he would handle this new issue surrounding Jim's medal. Wasting no time, once the boy joined him, he started in, "Tell me the truth, Johnny. Where'd you get that medal?"

He waited for the boy's answer, prepared to sit in front of the school the rest of the day. Teachers and children who stayed late, filtered out of the buildings, one by one. Passing by the truck, they each glanced at Walter Henry, which made him feel more uncomfortable. He was a patient man, but he grew frustrated, especially with the boy's reply.

"You gave it to me."

Johnny was the smallest in his class, though two years older than the eldest of them. Nearly fourteen years of age, and often called, "puny," he scarcely recognized that he was on the verge of manhood. One of Walter Henry's old shirts served as his jacket, sleeves always rolled up. His light-brown hair had grown shaggy, gaping holes in his pants revealed his knees, and stains showed on his clothes. But, the all-important truth, a secret about which he recently became aware, rose highest in his estimation, much higher than the shirt on his back.

Walter Henry saw Johnny gripping the medal as if it might fly away. It displayed the Edenville High School colors and even the year Jim graduated from high school. Given to Jim upon graduation for leading the football team to victory, it honored him for representing their school proudly, in sports and in academics. The old blacksmith was torn between his feelings of pride that day years ago, when Jim placed the medal around his grandmother's neck as a gift, and the current issue, when he needed to teach Johnny a difficult lesson. Many mistakes were made in his lifetime and, though this one would not be his worst, it was nearly so.

"I never gave that to you."

Johnny's hand went for the door handle as he shouted, "Yeah, you did! It was in the lunch sack you gave me! You said I could have everything in it!" His underhanded claim was taking the matter too far, but Johnny was too upset and angry to give up now.

Walter Henry painfully recalled the lunch Rosa left at the barn...a special lunch she made for Jim.

With eyes closed, one rainy day returned to punish him for daring to get old and becoming remiss in his duties as adopted father for more than one young man. The day they cleared Ev Mendoza's house, Jim obsessively sifted through the muck and debris, purposefully searching for anything of value. The medal Johnny clasped within his grip, and which meant the whole world to him—

"It wasn't mine to give you." Walter Henry put his hand out, palm up, in front of the boy. "It doesn't belong to us. It's Jim's medal." The boy refused to cooperate, so Walter Henry applied some pressure. "Now, I'm your father—"

"*You're not my father!!*"

Johnny bolted from the truck and ran down the street. Walter Henry got out and yelled after him. He ran as far as he could, but was soon out of breath and needed to stop. Looking all around, it dawned on him that Johnny disappeared.

• • •

Rosa was in the kitchen when she saw her mother outside on the front steps, pushing her sweaty hair away from her forehead, looking exhausted. Disappointed, she set the wedding planner aside, missing her grandmother again. Earlier, Patty McGrew tried talking her into letting others help with the wedding, others like Patty, who had the money, the time, and the strength to do it. But, Rosa insisted, "No, I want my mother to help."

Patty pointed out to her, "You don't understand, Rosa. Your mother's been through too much."

"I know. And, now—" Rosa stopped herself from bringing up her brother's problems. "You're right," she admitted and began to cry.

Getting married was emotional business for Rosa. Her mother helped in small ways, making a guest list and a menu, but they were mere scraps of paper she swiftly tucked inside the wedding planner. Her friend, Coco, who agreed to be matron of honor, planned to help with the bridesmaid's dresses. Getting together to sew, they agreed, was happily reminiscent of their high school days. Rosa, however, needed to face facts. A wedding involved much more than some lists and a few dresses could solve. Even so, she wanted to give her mother a chance.

"Sure, honey." Patty gave Rosa a warm hug. "Let me know what your mother says. That way I can tell Daddy about it and start making arrangements."

She was ecstatic, but restrained herself, waiting for Rosa to give her the okay. She began cleaning the beauty salon before she closed for the day. Unable to contain herself, she declared, "This will be the best wedding this town has ever seen!" She was so excited, yet secretly hoped her own daughter waited a few more years before she got married. "But...wouldn't it be nice?" She imagined Dottie and Rosa, both in white dresses. "A double wedding!" Chuckling, she warned herself, "Better not! Daddy would have a *coronary!*"

Reaching to pull down the window shade, she saw Johnny walking into town. He presented a pitiful sight, clothes all bedraggled and dirty, wandering down the street like a lost dog. She noticed he wore something familiar around his neck. She hurried outside and hailed him, "Johnny! Where's your dad?"

He didn't answer.

She quickly locked the door and rushed to catch up to him. "Johnny! Where're you goin', son?" She worried about him, appearing despondent, ignoring her, it seemed. He continued sauntering along until he entered the diner. Patty waved her hand through the air to dismiss it. "Oh, his dad's probably there," she said, and chuckled to herself again, eager to get back to her wedding daydreams.

Later that evening, Rosa telephoned Patty while her mother was in the bathroom running the bath water. She tried to keep her voice down, in case her mother really did have super hearing. "I'm not sure this is a good time to talk to my mother about the wedding, Patty. She's not feeling well today."

Alluding to her encounter with Johnny, Patty commented, "Hmm, I think that might be goin' around." She told Rosa about seeing the boy in town, walking along in a daze, like he was sick.

"Johnny?" Rosa failed to understand what Johnny Henry had to do with anything until Patty told her.

"He was wearing one of those medals they give graduates at the high school, like the one Buster got for wrestling, remember? I wonder where he got it from."

Rosa knew immediately and said a quick goodbye. No matter how tired and sick her mother was, Rosa needed to talk to her. This was too important to ignore.

She called through the bathroom door, "Mom?"

Candelaria was sinking into the hot bath water and groaning softly. She answered, "What is it, Rosa? Can't it wait?" She was so tired and wanted only to be left alone.

"It's important, Mom! It can't wait!" She spoke gently, "At least once you get your bath. We need to talk."

"Okay."

Candelaria knew it must be important, so she took a short, soaking bath. Combing her hair, she opened the bathroom door, already in pajamas, robe, and slippers. Rosa was preparing dinner, canned peas and a salad, along with some leftover chicken-fried steak. She set a glass of milk in front of her, and a paper napkin. In a subdued manner, Candelaria thanked Rosa, sighing heavily before slowly eating everything on her plate.

Rosa considered how much her mother needed the income she earned working at the beauty parlor. Though not enough to live on, by itself, it provided the means for her and her mother to live in their own home, be fed, and buy the minimum of necessities. Her mother's small income, from doing farm work, constituted a lesser, though greatly needed portion of their total income. What would her mother do once she got married? Rosa often wondered, wishing she could address the issue with her brother, Jim.

Rosa wondered what to do, now that Johnny had Jim's medal she carelessly left with Walter Henry at the blacksmith shop. She recalled the exact location of where the medal was kept at her grandmother's house, carefully draped across a little scrapbook, displayed on a shelf with other mementos. Rosa became more upset, because these precious items comprised Jim's graduation gift to their grandmother. She assumed the scrapbook must have burned in the fire.

She washed the few dishes, prepared to go into the small living room to talk, but her mother gave a quiet good night and retired to her bedroom. Rosa followed her, raising her voice in frustration, "Mom! We were going to talk, remember?!" When she opened the door and saw her mother sitting on the edge of the bed, head in hands, she instantly felt terrible. Deciding to skip the discussion on Jim's medal, she sat beside her mother, affectionately wrapping her arm around her. Candelaria got under the covers and Rosa kissed her forehead, saying, "I love you, Mom."

The evening yet early, Rosa dashed into town to address the issue on her own. Once there, she spotted Johnny sitting by himself in a booth at the diner, looking forlorn. He removed the medal and, when she walked in, talking so gently to him, he buried his head in his arms on the table. He set the medal down, along with the scrapbook, dejectedly pushing them aside. Surprised to see the little photo album, Rosa quickly composed herself and sat beside the boy. Gently pulling his arms up and away from the table, with all the love she had to give, she drew her own arms around him in a warm embrace.

Johnny closed his eyes and let Rosa hold him in her arms. The medal lay on the table with the scrapbook, having dwindled in stature into meaningless, blackened relics found in a burned down, old house. He no longer wanted them, though he could not tell Rosa so, for he came to know the truth and was, himself, bereft with sorrow. His real mother and father were gone from the world, and he grieved in his heart, because it might as well be true, for all he mattered.

Coming down with the same illness Candelaria had, Johnny could no longer follow the course he had taken since Ev Mendoza's house burned. He should have given the scrapbook to Jim the moment he discovered it, months ago. If he had given Walter Henry the medal he found in the lunch sack, this devastating experience would never have happened. It was too late for that now, but he knew what he could do. He could go home to the man who adopted him, who never let him down, never walked away from him, never—

The bell on the diner door jingled as Walter Henry walked in and stopped, seeing Rosa with Johnny. Millie came out of the back room and also stopped. Tears filled her eyes, looking at Walter Henry, then at the boy. Once Rosa stepped out of the booth, Johnny hurried past her and ran to Walter Henry, hugging him and apologizing.

"I'm sorry! I made a mess of things, didn't I?"

Rosa quietly left the diner, planning to drive to the livery stable, hoping her brother was still at work.

Earlier, when Johnny ran away, Walter Henry searched everywhere, calling out the boy's name and asking people if they saw him. When he checked the livery stable, Jim was gone. The doors were open and a pitchfork lay neglected on the ground. He worried about the man, suspecting Johnny immediately turned to him in his crisis. Unfortunately, unable to do anything for the older of the two, he left the barn. He needed to find his son, at least the boy he called his son, praying he was all right.

"Well, Johnny, I think I've made a mess of things, too. I could have handled it better."

Johnny informed him he gave Rosa the medal and the scrapbook he found. Walter Henry hugged the boy, not so little after all.

"I should have taken the time to work it out with you."

Turning his attention toward Millie, standing there so patiently, the time came for him to share his feelings for her. The words he needed to say were not easy for him. He could at least show her, so he opened his arms to her. Without hesitation, she went to him and they embraced.

Sharing in their love, Johnny, Walter Henry, and Millie May Forester became a family. Johnny needed that more than anything, more than a medal or a scrapbook, or even wishing and hoping could provide. He forgave Walter Henry, the man who raised him and, in his heart, where his dream yet dwelled, he silently forgave his real parents, because they could not.

CHAPTER SIXTEEN

Sylvia Sumner silently pushed her shopping cart past Rosa Hart, pretending to decide which brand of chili to buy, even though it aggravated her husband's digestive problems. She wore a nylon fabric dress she ordered through a catalog. Pale violet with puffed sleeves and a pleated skirt, it sported a row of fake diamond buttons, sewn down the front, between the collar and waistline. Seeing Rosa on this rare occasion, reminded her of Jim. She debated whether to tell Rosa that her brother was in trouble. He was drinking heavily. Despite her fear of how Jim might react, she took a chance and spoke to her.

"Rosa? Is that you?"

Anxious to speak to Sylvia about Jim, Rosa cut short her foolish pretense over which cans of soup to buy. "Yes, it's me. Sylvia...Sumner, right?"

Rosa had not seen Sylvia up close since high school. Her eyes, an unusual, smoky, bluish shade of gray, remained her most striking feature. An especially pretty woman, it was common knowledge that men in town found her attractive, Jim included. That last thought made Rosa extremely uncomfortable. Sylvia and her brother's history was a long and emotional one with which neither Rosa nor her mother ever came to terms. Although, she would have much preferred her to Beth as a sister-in-law, but—

"I like your outfit." Sylvia smiled radiantly, her eyes piercing.

Rosa wore fashionable, capri-style pants, zipper on the side, a light-green color, and her blouse was white with light-green polka dots. She returned Sylvia's compliment. "Oh, I love your dress." The darker violet shade of Sylvia's belt and high-heeled shoes matched it perfectly, she was sure to add.

"Your hair is darling." Sylvia's compliment referred to Rosa's new style, called a "flip."

Rosa liked Sylvia, which surprised her. Heedless of gossip, and the past, she asked, "Would you like to join me for coffee? There's a new cafe out on the highway I've been dying to try. My fiancé, Bus—uhh, Stephen, wants to take me out to dinner there, but I wanted to check the menu first. I'd love it if you'd come."

Soon, they were driving into the mountains. Mountain Mystery Cafe & Gift Shoppe appeared on the right. Rosa pulled in and parked at the furthest end of the building. They entered the cafe, laughing lightly and smiling over little things, two women hitting it off as friends. However, despite the innocuous subject matter of their conversation, they were unknowingly dipping into dangerous waters.

Rosa made light of her usual concerns regarding this woman. Uncharacteristically defiant, she let come what may, poor judgement, or not. Nevertheless, an unfortunate incident at her parent's house came to mind. It involved Sylvia and took place when they were all teenagers. She disregarded the thought with the assertion that it happened a long time ago.

They sat in a booth at the opposite end of the cafe, by a window overlooking the forest.

Immediately, being the only customers in the place, a waitress approached their table and gave them menus.

Rosa spoke up quickly, "Oh, we're only having coffee," and looked at Sylvia.

Not wanting to be rude, Sylvia kept quiet, even though she hoped to have dinner.

The waitress asked, "Wouldn't you like some pie to go with your coffee? It's fresh baked."

Rosa and Sylvia quickly smiled at each other and said, "Sure!"

The waitress left, soon returning with coffees and extras, two plates of warm apple pie, each with a scoop of vanilla ice cream on top, which was already melting. After more small talk over the menu, they were silent, looking out the window or around the restaurant. Rosa and Sylvia both tried to be polite, but the real reason for their meeting remained unsaid.

In an attempt to broach the subject, Sylvia complained about Forty. "My husband never takes me out to dinner. He's just an old fuddy-duddy."

Rosa tried to keep her comments to herself. How Sylvia ever ended up with Forty Sumner, baffled her. She tried holding her tongue, not wanting to get involved in their marital problems, but had to say something. Why else would she be—well, were the rumors true?

"Sylvia . . ." Rosa paused, before continuing, "I've heard awful rumors about you and my brother." She cringed, thinking to herself, "Oh, good *grief!* Did I really say *that?!*"

Suddenly very uneasy, Sylvia placed her hand on her neck to rub it as she turned away from Rosa. Her other hand grabbed her purse. She became terrified and began to shake uncontrollably, wanting to leave the restaurant.

Rosa gently placed her hand on Sylvia's wrist, quietly reassuring her, "I don't care if it's true or not." Few others sat in the cafe, so her voice seemed too loud. "But, if it is true—" She felt like she stepped into a big hole full of quicksand, rapidly sinking in deeper every second. Excusing herself, she said they should leave. She spoke impulsively to Sylvia walking swiftly beside her, "Oh! I like you, Sylvia. I don't know what's going on and it's not any of my business, but I'm worried about my brother, that's all." They paid the cashier and left the cafe without delay.

Once outside, Sylvia said she worried, too. Crossing the parking lot with Rosa, she talked louder, "I'm sorry, Rosa! I'm truly sorry! I'm so ashamed of myself! But, I-I don't know what else to do!"

They reached Rosa's car, glancing behind themselves as other cars pulled up and parked. Lowering their voices, they stood on the other side of Rosa's car beneath the trees.

Sylvia was shaking again, nearly in hysterics. "I don't want to see Jim anymore!" Struggling to contain her worries, she lied. "Oh, I don't care what people say, either." Nevertheless, determined to inform Rosa, she took a deep breath and impulsively blurted out, "But, Jim's been talking crazy!" She looked around. "I can't just stop seeing him now! I'm afraid he'll hurt himself! You know what I mean, don't you?"

Sylvia's revelation stunned Rosa, because she knew exactly what Sylvia meant. She closed her eyes, wondering what she had done. Sylvia was the one person she intentionally kept at a distance for years, ever since discovering the hugely emotional effect she had on her brother. Jim used to cut himself, but she assumed he must have outgrown it. Here she was, talking with the woman who triggered such behavior in him! Her mother used to blame Sylvia for Jim's problems, the knowledge of which only further upset Rosa, yet also stirred her to action.

"I'll go and see him." She tried to sound brave, but she knew her brother needed the help of someone from the infirmary where, unfortunately, Beth worked.

Neither of them were aware that Beth, herself, had taken Jim there on several occasions, whenever there was an emergency. Beth repeatedly urged her husband to seek help from a psychiatrist, but her impassioned pleas typically brought on a pained expression.

Remembering the medal and the scrapbook, Rosa told Sylvia, "I have some things of his I've been meaning to give him. I won't mention I saw you."

"Thank you, Rosa! Thank you!" Sylvia looked down at the ground. "I know I never should have done it. There isn't a day that goes by—" She left it at that. Her head was swimming somewhere far away by this time, almost in a daze. Leaning back against the car, she got a cigarette from her purse and lit it, something she rarely did in public. Inhaling deeply, she blew the smoke out and felt calmer. It was one of those things that came over her, wanting the world to disappear.

Needing a distraction, herself, Rosa directed her attention toward the forest. The wind blew through the pine needles, making such a peaceful sound, like a soft breath sighing over them. She wished the day was over, longing to be in the arms of her future husband. Starting to lose interest in helping Sylvia, she regretted how foolish she behaved. To think she could help anybody, she inwardly called herself a pretender. Yet, now in her thirties, she willingly accepted life's more difficult problems. She mentally affirmed that everyone needs to have someone to whom they can turn.

"Thank you, Sylvia, for being so open and honest with me."

Sylvia hugged Rosa. "Thank you, for treating me like a normal person."

When they drove away, Rosa noticed Walter Henry's truck parked in front of the restaurant. She wondered if he knew what was going on between Sylvia and her brother. No matter. Though she confirmed the rumors, details were not something she wanted to hear.

CHAPTER SEVENTEEN

Arriving at Sylvia's house, Rosa became terribly nervous, hoping to avoid seeing Forty. Too late, she saw him opening the door, watching her leave. Trying to ignore him, she inadvertently turned to go further down the road, instead of back the way she had come. She wanted to look for Jim at his workplace, not show up at his house, especially uninvited. Regardless of her mistake, she kept her eyes directed straight ahead, slowly turning down his driveway, as if she had intended to do so all along.

Carrying a bag of groceries, Sylvia whisked past Forty on her way into the house. He stepped outside to keep an eye on Rosa, focusing his attention solely upon her actions. Front teeth pressed down on his lower lip, the tip of his tongue pressing forward at the back of his top teeth, he attempted a whistle, but failed. All he accomplished was an intense, low, "pfssst!" He stealthily questioned himself in a low voice. "What have we here?" First, Rosa brings his wife home, and then goes to her brother's house? To even consider Rosa happened to offer Sylvia a ride home? Not Chester Ferguson! Nor Pierson Adleberry. He never saw Rosa so much as look at Sylvia, never talked to her. It all seemed very suspect to Forty, who knew immediately that foul play was afoot. Slowly, he edged his way along the porch and carefully sat in one of two upholstered chairs. One might think he was about to sit on a cactus, such was his care. But, he was concerned someone might hear or even see him. In the deepest shade, he patiently waited as night arrived in their quiet neighborhood.

Rosa turned on her headlights, advancing slowly toward Jim and Beth's house, the rocks on their driveway crunching beneath her tires. The car chassis bounced excessively across each dip in the road. Shep and Tessie came running up to do their job, barking and taking a stand in front of the house. Rosa planned to wait in the car, so she kept the engine running. When she rolled down the window to call Jim's name, the dogs leapt and bounded like overgrown puppies to her side of the car, sniffing her. She loved them, so gave up and turned off the engine and the headlights, and got out of the car.

Right away, they were jumping on her. "Down! Down!" They whined and wagged, licking her face when she bent down to hug each of them.

Jim came out the front door, extremely pleased to see his sister, excitedly laughing. Beth was at him again, nagging and questioning, until he was sick of it. When Rosa showed up, it offered the guilty man a welcomed escape.

"Hey, Rosa! It sure is good to see you!" He was overdoing it a bit, hugging her vigorously and playing with the dogs. "Hey, Shep! Hey, Tessie! Did Rosa come to see you two?"

Rosa noticed Beth standing by the door, looking her usual, unfriendly self, arms crossed in front of her and an odd, squinty-eyed sneer on her face. Hoping to limit the strange encounter, she climbed into the car to get her purse. She wanted to give the medal and the scrapbook to Jim right away, but he automatically got into the car.

He shouted to his wife, "Hey, Beth, I gotta show Rosa the horse we have over at the livery stable, all right?! I won't be long!"

Rosa said a quick and absentminded goodbye.

The disgruntled woman turned to re-enter the house, figuring her husband was safe as long as his sister was around. Nonetheless, she had to at least give a little shake of her head, closing the front door and laughing derisively at Jim's deceptive, yet foolish antics. Beth saw through his escape tactics. She laughed again. He was too easy, but she felt sorry for him, and a bit guilty, seeing Rosa. What a state the house was in! "Shoot! I better clean house!" She thought Rosa might also bring Jim home.

The dogs jumped into the car before Rosa could close the door, stomping all over her with their dirty, clawing paws. She tried to move herself out of their way, shoving them into the back seat. She fanned her hand through the air at their odor and shedding fur floating near her face.

Jim let out an excessively boisterous and loud, fitful kind of laugh, and said, "Hey! It's the whole family!"

Overwhelmed by the unnerving and totally unexpected commotion Jim and his dogs created, Rosa reminded herself Jim used to always behave rambunctious. The thought reassured her. Thankful for the opportunity to spend time with her brother, she started up the car, turned on the headlights, and swung around to drive to the barn. Her bouncy car drew more laughter out of Jim, who made himself comfortable, resting his arm on the door, slouching down in the car seat, with his other arm stretched out along the top of it.

The dog's tongues were lolling and dripping as they panted and bounced around.

"Man! You need to get your car fixed, Rosa! Why don't you have Buster take it down to the shop?" He laughed out loud some more and looked back at the dogs, petting and praising them. "Hey, Tess! That's a good girl. Good boy, Shep! Good boy!"

Still overwhelmed, Rosa imagined herself transporting a carload of young, teenaged boys, Jim included, jauntily setting out for their first ball game, only she regretted ever inviting them along. He acted like a fourteen-year-old, instead of— It seemed funny to her, because their father acted the same way, boisterous and energetic when he was happy and having fun. Remembering that, brought a smile to her face, so she welcomed the diversion, having never realized until then, that Jim behaved very much like their father.

In this way, able to lighten up, she said, "I can't afford to fix my car. I'm waiting for Buster and I to get married. We're going to get a new car!"

Turning onto the main dirt road, Rosa noticed Jim grow tense. Drawing near to Forty and Sylvia's house, she could imagine what caused this shift in his demeanor. "So much for conversation," she off-handedly remarked.

His attention fixed intently in the direction of the house coming up on the right, Jim feigned interest in Rosa's complaint. The sound of his voice lowered with an almost mocking undertone, "So...how is ole *Bus*ter? I haven't talked to him...since I switched hardware stores. Mr. Goodman raised his prices."

Rosa grew steadily uneasy. Jim's brooding state of mind gave her the chills. Listening to him, she wondered if he even liked her fiancé, or anyone. Recalling her visit with Sylvia, she worried what Jim might think if he knew they spent time together over coffee and pie, talking about *him!* She wished she never went to the cafe with Sylvia. She believed it was a terrible mistake. She watched the road and drove along as the dreaded house came into view.

Jim saw Sylvia's cigarette tip glow brighter. He wanted her to be his, for them to be together, to leave that place far behind.

Noting his moodiness, Rosa asked, "Everything okay, Jim?" She rolled her eyes, thinking that was a dumb question.

He answered her, though, "Yeah...it's just that neighbor of mine. Forty. He's getting too nosey."

Tempted to ask, "Can you blame him?" Rosa, nevertheless, played along with the evasion. She innocently brought up how she ran into Forty digging through their grandmother's destroyed home, unaware how significant the information would be to Jim.

Jerking around in his seat, he yelled, *"What?!"* He was furious.

Rosa recalled her brother's temper and how aggressive he could be at times, a fearsome reminder of his unpredictable mood swings. No longer a boy, his aggression had a very different effect on her now.

Regretfully, she went on to explain, "Yeah! I showed up at Grandma's the same morning her house burned down! The fire department was just barely leaving." She stopped in front of the livery stable.

Jim pressed the issue, "What the *hell* was Forty doing there?!" He opened the car door and, still angry, asked her, "Did you find anything?!"

She was relieved when he got out of the car, grateful for the opportunity to calm down.

He opened the back door and the dogs jumped out, while she shut off the engine and the headlights. Reluctantly, she got out of the car while he unlocked the barn. Approaching him, she reminded herself he was only her brother and followed him into the barn, barely able to see anything. He lit a lantern placed on the workbench. In that instant, Rosa could not recall why she wanted to see him. He was completely domineering the conversation. Out of her own fear and guilt, she became the little girl with bruised shins, angry and crying as her feisty little brother ran off to hide.

While they were both quiet, she tried to figure out how to talk to him. It helped to remind herself she was older than him. They were both older, for goodness' sake, supposing her discomfort was merely the result of their having grown apart. Although, she admitted, her uneasiness was most likely due to having very recently become Sylvia's confidant. Rosa regretted doing that, to believe she could simply chat over coffee with Jim's illicit lover, then drive over to have a heart-to-heart with him, anytime she wanted, as though she knew them. Yet, in a way, he was still the same, which gave her a feeling almost like pity. She matured and moved on, while here was Jim, still working at the family business, still living in their old house, and still dallying with Sylvia Cadwallader.

She decided not to talk to Jim on Sylvia's behalf, but she wanted to accomplish her other task. She picked up the conversation where they left off. "Oh, Forty? Same thing I was doing. Trying to find anything worth saving. It bothered me at first, but he's harmless. Kind of strange, yet harmless," adding to herself, "except when he's the husband of the woman you're having an affair with, you dope!"

Jim asked, "So, did you find anything?"

"Yeah. I found an old picture of Mom. Oh! And Forty found your old football medal!" She started to turn to get Jim's medal and the scrapbook out of her purse in the car, when Jim strode over to her in his rage, his hands balled into fists.

"You should have told him to leave!! He had no business being there!!"

She drew back, frightened at this change in him and yelled, "Jim! What's the *matter* with you?!" Incredulous and shocked, she demanded, "Why are you so angry?!" His outburst caught her way off guard.

Jim turned around and deliberately walked away from her, stepping further into the barn, rubbing his face and the back of his neck. He was having trouble controlling himself and wanted Rosa to leave. He believed it was for the best.

Rosa, herself, wanted to leave, but instead walked past him, stern, yet on the verge of tears, watching him out the corner of her eyes. Nearing the stalls, the horse Jim told her about, softly whinnied.

Attempting to change the subject, she said, "I came here to see the horse. Remember?" She needed time to collect herself. Stubbornly, she patted the Appaloosa, praising it, though she was still mad at Jim. She no longer wanted to give him the medal and the scrapbook, wishing they had burned in the fire. They caused enough trouble, she believed. She decided she was done playing the fool and told herself it was time to take charge of things. She was about to get married to a man. It was high time she learned to exert her womanly power!

"Listen here," she said in a decidedly assertive, though somewhat aggressive tone.

Stepping confidently out of the shadows, she moved into the lighted area of the barn.

Surprised, Jim looked at her. He never saw his sister behave this way. She was fearless. No longer was she the fashionable young beautician. She was strong, mature, and wise. Jim responded to her confidence, his voice softening, as he asked, "Rosa?" He was her little brother again, back when he looked up to her and she was protective of him, even taking care of him. His bitterness fell away, replaced by an overriding, deep feeling of sorrow, mixed with an honest respect for his sister. He became hopeful, needing her. Feeling ashamed, he revealed himself to her, the teenaged boy who yearned to be freed of his suffering.

Rosa never wanted to argue with him, nor hurt him, definitely not put him down. She loved her brother and cared deeply about him, knowing what he had been through as a child. When she came fully into the soft, lantern light, she read him, picking up on his vulnerability.

Relaxing, she looked around the barn, giving herself more time, gradually drawing closer to him. The interior of the barn was noticeably different than when their father was alive, tidy and clean, for a barn. Although she respected her brother's privacy, she desperately needed to talk with him about real things, real issues. At the same time, she also wanted to leave, for the day to be at an end.

Jim spoke first. "I'm sorry, Rosa, for jumping all over you about my neighbor." He shook his head, grabbed a stool for each of them to sit on, and calmly went on, "Seems like ever since Dad died...I've been mad at the whole world." His head hung down and his lower chin began to quiver.

Without hesitation, Rosa went to him, sitting on the stool he provided for her and wrapping her arms around him, holding him.

He suddenly sank in strength and willpower, dropping into her arms. His sobs came in bursts, at first. From somewhere deep within himself, a force upwelled, and he choked and gasped in loud, outright sobbing. He was the young man fresh out of high school, the son who lost his father before he had the chance to say goodbye, before he could prove himself to his dad.

Rosa knew that boy well, seeing him through her grown-up eyes, feeling so much love for him. Closing her eyes, she prayed without words, simply loving her brother. She felt sorry for herself, too, for neither of their lives were easy. Jim's life turned out very differently from her own, for other reasons she considered herself fortunate enough to escape. Unable to undo the past, all she could do was in the moment. In the golden-hued lantern light, the shadows held at bay in the corners of the barn, she held a soul in her care, a tormented soul nearing its last days as Jim Hart.

CHAPTER EIGHTEEN

The sun rose brightly over the mountains. Its slanting rays filtered downward through the trees to the small valley below. A light mist emanated from shrinking pools of water where bullfrogs called in deep, booming bellows, like belches from the water's muddy depths. People left their homes for work or for school, a small, but steady exodus going toward quaint shops and long-established businesses. Sidewalks were busily swept by aproned shopkeepers. A distant tractor started up to plow a field. The dingy yellow school bus cranked to a stop to let high school students climb aboard, the girls with their books held close, the boys with theirs slung carelessly by their side. The bus rocked and creaked as they boarded, the door clunked shut, and the driver strained the gears to get the old beast moving forward, chugging along once more. Women waved goodbye to their husbands, dressed in suits or in overalls. Some of the wives had sparkling eyes, others looked on with relief. They had their own work to do, patching and mending, cleaning and scrubbing, sweeping and tidying and cooking and— Somewhere in the midst of it all, a shot rang out.

Fortuitous Sumner, self-appointed town detective and private investigator, had his recently pilfered gun repaired. The owner of the gun shop happened to have some bullets.

"It's gotta be more than fifty, maybe sixty years old," he said.

Behind his shop, he maintained a private, target practice area. Across a barren stretch of mud, a cardboard man, propped in front of a stack of hay bales, awaited them. Off in the shade beneath an oak tree, the red bullseye on the threatening figure, stood out clearly. The store owner showed Forty how to use the gun, encouraging him to try it out. It worked well enough, the shopkeeper told him, with the added reminder, "It's not a toy!"

Placing a few extra bullets in a small envelope, he sealed it and carefully set it in a small, wooden gun collector's box. After tucking in some padding, he placed the unloaded gun inside, carefully sliding the top of the box in place before handing it to his eager and awe-inspired customer.

Happier than ever, Forty returned to work. Eyes wide, he vividly imagined what the gun could do for him. When Rosa brought Sylvia home, he grabbed the gun and stuck it in the back of his pants. Unfortunately, he missed the waistband! The gun slipped down into his drawers. Gingerly, yet with no time to lose, he retrieved it before going outside to sit. Watching and waiting, he remained alert to Rosa's return.

Sylvia sat with him, smoking a cigarette, which Forty detested. He was hungry and wanted some dinner. Furthermore, he wanted her respect. Hunkering down in the dark, he held the gun in his hand, his Bible close by on a small, wooden table. Sylvia occasionally knocked the ash on her cigarette into an ashtray on that same table. Seeing the two objects fading into the unseeing-ness of night, his trusted Bible and Sylvia's fingertip tapping the end of her cigarette, gave Forty the oddest feeling.

To him, it summed up everything he knew to be true, though he could not put it into words. When the night grew darker and he could no longer see the table before him, all that remained were his awkward feelings and the gun he securely held.

No streetlights shone near their home. Night arrived like a fog of black obscurity. The stars barely glimmered, far beyond the reach of the tallest of trees. Scurrying rustlings of wildlife foraging in the woods, disturbed the stillness. An owl roosting nearby sent out its boom! Boom! Or, so its hooting sounded to those two who watched and waited, uncaring of stars and stirring wildlife. A great draft of wind carried aloft a chorus of barking dogs around the neighborhood and the rich, greasy odor of hamburger meat frying.

Forty breathed a sigh of relief, thankful that dinner was cooking. Instantly alert, he thought he heard Rosa's approaching automobile and Jim's gleeful laughter. Soon, they were driving past in her jostling vehicle. Jim sat slouched in the front seat, looking intently at their house, a sight which Forty believed he must have imagined.

The following morning, he could hardly wait to try out the gun on his own target. He drew a hasty bullseye on a piece of paper and tacked it to a tree in their weedy backyard.

Sylvia came out to sit on the porch steps, still in her nightgown and robe, sipping some coffee. She piped up, "You're gonna be late for work." Despite her disinterested tone, she was curious about Forty's new interest in this gun, turning up out of nowhere. "Where'd you get that old thing?"

She soon became annoyed with him, not answering her question, ignoring her. Forty used to be one of her closest childhood friends, along with their neighbor, Tucker Stewart. She once loved them both and dearly revered those days when life was no more challenging than choosing what candy to spend a nickel on or where to play that day. She wondered whatever happened to the red-headed little boy who used to wet his pants. They tried to cheer their little friend, the most timid of their loyal troupe, while Mrs. Stewart gave him clothes to wear after Forty bathed at their house. She washed his shorts and underwear, even his shirt and socks. Meanwhile, they lay on their stomachs on the living room floor, taking turns reading the comics.

Forty always grew excited. "I wanna read Dick Tracy!" He said that every time.

Sylvia remembered exchanging glances with Tucker. They smiled at one another for being kind to Forty. Sylvia pretended they were the parents, fondly looking on, and Forty was their child, happily reading the funnies.

Innocently continuing her mental wandering into the past, one day in particular came to mind. She and Forty mysteriously became the children. Tucker was the grown up, herself only eleven, while he was twelve. "Going on thirteen," he was sure to stress. Forty was sick that day, unable to meet them at their fort.

"Hey, Syl," Tucker called to her, a nickname only he and Jim Hart used.

Sylvia half-turned toward him, smiling sweetly. "Yeah?"

He slowly strode toward her and stood close. Hopeful he still wanted to spend the day with her, she waited. Behaving especially tender, he leaned over to kiss her on the lips in the shade of the trees behind Forty's parent's house.

She laughed a little, more like a delightful giggle, and asked, "What was that for?"

He blushed and acted annoyed, rolled his eyes, though answered her honestly, "Because I like you, silly!"

Sylvia was pleased. "I like you, too," she said.

Pow! The shot rang out, shaking Sylvia out of her reverie, scattering an explosion of flight, birds scattering from the treetops. Dogs began barking in response.

Forty inspected the target, disappointed there was no hole to be found. He looked over at the porch, to see if his wife witnessed his poor aim, seeing her coffee cup on the ground. Impatient with her, and embarrassed, he tore the target off the tree and went inside the house.

"Sylvia?!" He shouted up the stairs, "I'm gonna go to work now!" He waited for her answer. Still impatient, he went up the stairs, finding her in the bedroom, pacing the floor. Seeing her so agitated, he instantly calmed down and tenderly apologized to her, "Sweetheart. I'm sorry," he said, and put his arms around her.

Sylvia rested her head on his shoulder and cried. She still loved him.

He gently repeated himself, "I'm gonna go to work."

She nodded, her handkerchief in hand, held close to her face.

Forty regretted upsetting his wife. He promised himself never to harm Sylvia the way his father harmed his mother. Forty promised his mother, "When I grow up, I'm gonna take you far away where no one can hurt you anymore." He knelt by the bed where his mother lay, crying, after his father stormed off to work in an angry tempest.

"Now you stay *put!*" His father's fat finger jabbed the air before his glaring scowl swept over them. Glancing quickly at Forty, he said, "And, that goes for the both of you!" The house shook when his father slammed the door, the windows rattling like a shudder, such was the force of his departing presence.

Forty asked his mother, "Why does Daddy hate us?"

Blandly, she answered, "I don't know."

On his way to work, Forty reminded himself to have another talk with his wife. He dreaded the idea of it. In contrast, he relished the thought of having a talk with his neighbor, maybe use his gun for added emphasis. Impulsively, he pounded the steering wheel with his fist, anticipating a confrontation. "Lying cheat! I'll give you what for, Stewart! You can't get away with stealing my wife from me!" He made a pretend gun, folding in his fingers and pointing his index finger, then fired it out the windshield of his convertible. "Shoo-wee!" He added the whistle he was practicing. With the car top down, Forty breezed on down the road through Edenville, lost in his fantasy about gunning down his neighbor.

• • •

Sylvia stood by their bedroom window watching Forty leave. The emptiness of his departure left within her view the yellowed lace curtains and an unswept wood floor. She dared not look at the bed behind her, where she and Forty slept side by side, and where the squeaking springs could still be heard when last he wanted—

She dressed and was soon heading out the back door. Looking for Jim, she took the alleyway behind her house, crossing the road, going behind the brick buildings of Pine Way. Stepping carefully, so as not to dirty her shoes or get damp from the tall grass along the path, she passed behind the old general store. Noticing the open sliding door and the sculptor inside, busy at work beneath a shower of flaring sparks, she paused. Fearful the middle-aged man might see her, she swiftly walked past. Between familiar stones where grass grew the shortest, she tiptoed quickly until she reached the back of the barn. Its weathered boards, grayed and splintered, appeared like home to her, where so often she waited by its side, and where so many times she had fallen.

Admiring the trees nearby, she appreciated the morning light, only a glimmer in the highest branches. Father Jovial's words came to mind, "Adultery is a sin, little Miss," which is what he said to her mother. Sylvia played close enough to the house that day, she could hear them talking. He stood at the front door, speaking privately with her mother. The only thing Sylvia truly learned from the encounter, that he cared, she held dear.

To her relief, Jim came outside with something in his hand to wash in the sink. She waited, fearful of the truth she fought daily. She told Forty, "no," again. Seeing her, Jim tossed the item into the sink and rushed to meet her. Hand in hand, they dashed into the barn.

Their brazen conduct caught someone else's attention. Walter Henry saw them, pulled off his gloves, slapped them on the workbench, and marched directly out the front entrance.

"I need some air," he said.

CHAPTER NINETEEN

If Ev Mendoza was alive, she would not be surprised at the change in her daughter's family. The worst, she would say, took place the day her son-in-law died. He was killed by a rogue stallion that killed once before. Approaching the gray horse in the corral, her daughter, Candelaria, begged him to listen, but he grew more determined to do what others warned was purely suicidal.

The horse's hooves were deformed from neglect, its coat and tail matted and filthy. Open sores, from repeatedly ramming the corral fence were left untreated. Rope in hand, Candelaria's husband planned to lead the horse to the stable, trim its hooves and groom it, but Jimmy's efforts had tragic consequences. The pathetic creature did not live by horsemen's rules. It was not a wild horse, but it was a deadly one. Without a single chance of succeeding, Candelaria's husband stepped into the corral and closed the gate. The stallion charged, galloping straight toward him with one aim, to attack and to kill.

When the foreman of the stables heard what his friend, Jimmy Hart, planned to do, he rushed to the corral, but was too late. Fed up with the despicable animal, he grabbed the rifle from his truck cab and shot the stallion dead. Every person, who was not moving as fast as they could, was fixed in place, stunned in plain horror. When the horse dropped to the ground, Candelaria ran to her husband's side where he lay, his head crushed, his arms limp and twisted like a fallen puppet's, the master's hand no longer animating them. The owner of the horse, a renowned braggart and bully, and no friend of Jimmy Hart's, was unequivocally disturbed by what he saw.

Poor Ev noticed the decline of their house, soon after her daughter and son-in-law moved into the old Smith homestead. She tried her best to continue caring for her grandchildren, as she had done when they lived with her. But, her grandson had too much of his father's fearless side and not enough of his integrity and inner strength. Ev's mother-in-law, Lucy Shoseegan, forewarned her one day, when they were in the garden picking tomatoes. Jim and Rosa were playing nearby with that sweet little boy, Tucker, who would sometimes come down to the newspaper office with his father. They began fighting over something. Her grandson went after the other boy with fists balled up, ready to slug him in the face. He never reached his target. Ev managed to stop him, by lifting his kicking, thrashing body off the ground and carrying him into the house. The experience left her bruised in body, and in soul. Her mother-in-law said she detected in him the same ill temper she saw in Candelaria, a hot-headed rage as ferocious as a lion. Ev knew Candelaria's temper well, and witnessed it many times, trying each time to get her to calm down. She saw the same thing in her grandson, Jim.

Ev never forgot Lucy's words: "Those two, they have warrior spirits, ready to fight. But, they need discipline, someplace to direct it. They are like caged lions pacing their cells, longing only to be free."

Guilt, worry, and fear were ever present as Ev watched Jim grow. He never did much good at anything until he went out for football in high school. His popularity soared and his confidence grew. It turned out, he was a natural leader, made team captain in his senior year. Subsequently, his father's confidence in his son grew, so he began to place more and more responsibility on his son's shoulders. He often talked about Jim taking over the family business one day. Jim's coach and his teachers were preparing him for college, to go away, to leave home. Regardless, proud of his son and eager to teach him, Jimmy Hart methodically and patiently instructed him on everything he knew about their business. Ev believed her son-in-law neglected to teach Jim how to be a man out in the world, to be a good husband and, perhaps, a loving father.

The timing of his father's death could not have been worse, shortly after Jim graduated. He received a football scholarship from a prestigious state university, the first in his family to have this opportunity. Though he started dating Beth, he was also seeing Sylvia on occasion. His father and mother agreed, Beth was no good for him, but they also knew Sylvia was not only "as loose as a bushel of ladybugs," the way Jimmy once described her, she was plainly dangerous for their son to so much as notice. After her son-in-law's death, Ev caught Beth sneaking liquor from her son-in-law's cabinet, lying to Ev, saying Jim's parents let them drink. When she told her daughter, Candelaria packed it up in a fury, along with anything else reminding her of her husband, snatching up clothing, his guns, his toiletries, and even food from the refrigerator.

She was on a rampage, hauling it to the dump where she set it on fire, about which Ev had no idea. In absolute terror, what she did see was Candelaria dragging her son along with her, forcing him to get into the car. Ev was shouting after her to stop, running down the porch steps, thinking Rosa was following close behind, only to learn that her granddaughter had gone to her room to scream.

Ev never heard what happened once her daughter went charging up the driveway. Jim braced his hands on the door and the dashboard of their car as his mother fishtailed the vehicle out to the road. Once they reached the dump, still in a blind and reckless madness, Candelaria made Jim watch as she piled everything, throwing it out of the trunk onto the ground. He tried to grab his father's guns and his father's cologne, his father's coat, but she yanked him away from it and began squirting lighter fluid on the heap, setting it ablaze.

He yelled at her, "What are you doing this for?!! No!! *No!!*"

"Your father is dead! He isn't here anymore! *He left us!! He left us!! He left us!!*" She fell to her knees, sobbing, her hair resembling a lion's bushy mane as her head fell backward, arms flailed. Giving herself up to God, she silently pleaded with Him to save her, to have mercy.

Jim knelt beside his mother, holding her, the fierce, black lioness, soothing her, reassuring her. Calmly and quietly, he said, "I'll stay home, Mom. I won't go away. I'll take care of you and Rosa. Beth and I will get married. You'll see, Mom. Everything's going to be okay. I promise." At that moment, a dense cloud passed overhead, temporarily blocking the sun's light. Jim cast his eyes skyward as the shadow drifted onward, the sun's rays shining forth, brighter than ever.

He got up to retrieve the guns, untouched by the fire, while his mother sat slumped and unmoving. Gathering other items, like a bottle of his father's cologne, he decided to take everything to the livery stable, sparing his mother the haunting grief of their presence. However, no one was spared the heavy-laden stench wrought from smoldering food and clothing. They carried the reeking odor home with them, clinging to pained regrets and emanating from disparate glances toward Ev and Rosa.

Ev witnessed the family change, Jim and Beth taking over his parent's house and Candelaria moving into Villa Boracho. She would lament, "Ay, Dios mio." She prayed for them, but was reassured when Candelaria and Rosa seemed to fit in well, neighbors helping neighbors in a close-knit, family community. She noticed it took some pressure off of Jim, and thought, perhaps, things would be okay after all. To her dismay, she caught Jim taking notice of the pretty woman with the gray eyes, who dressed like she came straight out of the flapper era or a silent movie. Ev knew who Sylvia's parents were, but she never met them or talked to them, or to Sylvia's Aunt Justice. Wondering why her grandson would look at another woman that way, she warned Jim it was foolish, what he was doing, but he feigned misunderstanding.

It was Ev who rocked him to sleep when his mother and father worked long hours. It was she who held him as he spilled out his tears about being teased at school, kids calling him a "dirty Mexican." It was she who taught him to dance when he went to the homecoming dance. Ev loved him like her own son. She also loved Rosa, but Rosa did not have the troubles Jim experienced. Though she was emotional at times, Ev did not bond with her granddaughter the way she had with her grandson. He won her heart the first time she held him, right after he was born.

When she was dying and sorry about somebody not going away to college, she was trying to say, "I'm sorry, I should have told you to let Jim go away to college," for Ev had carried her daughter's mistake like it was her own. It no longer mattered. Those days were gone, and Ev was gone with them.

CHAPTER TWENTY

Candelaria never forgot her failings as a mother. But, she strived to triumph over the past, to nurture her dream and her gifts. She saw the lion, herself, one night, and when they joined in the march the previous year. They were in good spirits and excited when they first arrived, but soon shrank in awe over the sheer numbers. Converging on the state capitol, came the shouting throng of protestors, Mexican-Americans, Chicanos, Brown Berets, and women dressed like men with their hair cut in a man's flat-top style. The sleeves of their shirts were rolled up to hold their smokes or show off their tattoos. Candelaria saw women dressed like herself, like Esther, Rosa, and Coco, but she could not help but notice those rough-looking women eyeing them like men, berating them, telling them to go home, back to the kitchen, and asking, "Where's your apron, honey?" Those comments infuriated Candelaria and, as the crowd swelled in size, tempers rose, passions ignited by those with megaphones, shouting and chanting, *We have rights! We have rights! We have rights!*

On and on, the crowd pressed in, moving like one body toward the steps of the capitol building. Candelaria was beginning to panic. She lost track of Rosa, trying to see around her and trying not to get crushed. It was too much for her, unaccustomed to crowds. One mass of bodies pushed on her from every direction until she began to push back to get some room.

Something came forth from within her. It was the anger that destroyed her husband's memory, ripped away her mourning cloak, and hacked away at her hair. That which remained, she espied in her reflection that night, a fierce black lion with its mane like a symbol of its power, its eyes like golden fire. Here, it revealed itself again and, before Esther could reach her, Candelaria acted. She pushed her way through the crowd. People moved aside, their eyes wide, watching her appear to grow larger before their very sight.

Forward she went, people helping her to get through, up the steps, even handing her a megaphone. But, someone she never saw again after that day, led her to the podium where the lead speakers were assembling to address everyone. Eyes alight, her mother's memory and stories, her grandmothers' teachings, and their grandmothers, including the lineage of native blood, like a river flowing in her veins, began issuing forth. She heard in her awareness the songs of her grandmothers, but it was Candelaria's voice ringing true and being heard by everyone. Only briefly did she speak, but what she said was remembered by all who heard.

She shouted into the microphone, "Listen to me! I know who you are! I hear you!"

They began to pay attention to her, those with megaphones becoming silent as others pointed toward the podium.

Candelaria was shaking from a power filling her as she went on, "You are the voices of the oppressed and the dishonored, whose very right to be in this country, to live and to work here, has been denied through resentment, hatred, fear, and prejudice." She paused, looking around at the faces directed her way, everyone quiet. "I have also been oppressed, my voice gone unheard. I have lived with the put-downs, the name-calling, and disrespect for having brown skin and for being Mexican."

Something shifted in her again and she awoke to the dancing spirits in colored buckskin that encircled her, each dancer wearing a different color of the rainbow, their braided hair swinging and flying out. They threw their heads back in a native yell. She did not know what to do except to let herself speak until she could say no more.

"I cannot earn enough money doing farm work, to live off of, or have a decent place to sleep at night. The farmworkers housing is broken-down and drafty." She paused, then continued speaking, "But, let me tell you something!" She shouted out the words of her grandmother, "To be Mexican means to be Spanish *and* it means to be Indian. And it is the Indian in me speaking to you today, because it is the Indian in us all that has been murdered and oppressed for *centuries!* And it is the native spirit striving today to claim what is rightfully ours!"

She calmed down and finished her speech. "We are not just Mexican. We are Mexican-*Americans*. We work hard to earn a living and to feed our families! We contribute to this country and to its economy! We deserve, *no*, we have a *right* to be heard *here*, today, and *tomorrow*, and *every* day!" She quieted, waiting and scanning the crowd, seeing hope on each person's face, looking up at her in expectation. "I know who you are. You are my people. We are *all* Mexican-*Americans*. We are Native *Americans*. We are *true* Americans!"

The crowd cheered and applauded. Candelaria took up the chanting, herself, as her grandmothers sang in her heart. "We have rights! We have rights! We have rights! Are we gonna let anyone take them away?!"

The crowd roared, "*No!!*"

The black lion disappeared as enigmatically as it had come forth. Candelaria slipped away to find Rosa and the others, the fire in her eyes cooling, the lion satisfied, for now.

Rosa and Coco did not join the march all the way to the capitol. When the protesters began pressing in and the numbers grew, Rosa shouted to her mother and to Esther, saying they were going to wait in the car for them. Esther heard and acknowledged it, but Candelaria, by then, was swept along in the tide of moving bodies. Esther kept her eye on Candelaria, even as her friend mounted the steps of the capitol and took the podium. Her mouth hung open in awe of her sister-friend of whom she was so proud, that her heart burned until tears filled her eyes and streamed down her face. She cried in joy for Candelaria, whom she now knew would no longer banish her dreams to take care of her children who, in truth, no longer needed her care. Rosa was beginning to turn to her future husband, to rely on him, while Jim was beyond her reach. For whatever purpose, Esther believed that God would not allow Candelaria to intervene in Jim's life.

Everyone who heard Candelaria that day were filled with love and pride, hope uplifting them. Other speakers followed, culminating with the leaders of the Chicano Movement, farmworkers' union organizers, Brown Berets, and supporters. It was a day to go down in history as the beginning of a new era for Mexican-Americans. Not only were they hopeful, supported, heard, and organized, they were empowered to speak, to lend their voices to the changing tide through song, poetry, articles, lectures, and other forms of artistic expression. Candelaria would be among the writers telling the world the story of a people, continuing on a legacy of storytelling for Mexican-American and Native American authors who followed in their footsteps.

"Thank God, I made them dress proper." Esther nodded in agreement with herself as she hailed her *new* friend, Candelaria Mendoza Hart, who appeared about eight feet tall to her and so impressive. "Laria! Laria! Over here!" Esther had her hand in the air, waving at Candelaria. When they finally met, Esther's smile was tremendous.

Candelaria asked her, "Where's Rosa?! I lost sight of her!" She was trying not to shout, pushing against the crowd, people looking at her as though they wanted to always remember her. Some thanked her, while others quickly hugged.

One of the women with a butch haircut, in men's chino pants and t-shirt, stopped Candelaria, put one hand on her shoulder, and shook her hand with the other. "Hey, thank you, Sister." She was praising Candelaria, patting her shoulder. "You were amazing. What you said." She withdrew her hands and let Candelaria move along, stepping back away from her. She shouted, "Hey! You've changed my mind about the ladies! You're my hero!"

Before Esther and Candelaria could go back to the car, they took some time to sit on a bench on the capitol grounds. They hugged some more and Candelaria told Esther what she planned to do.

"I'm going to write down everything I've learned from my life, from my mother, and my grandmother." Her voice breaking and her eyes full of the tears of her dreams, she went on, "I'm going to begin with this day and go from there. I don't know who will want to read it, but, if this crowd is any indication, I know they'll want to."

She threw her arms around her friend. "Oh, Chavie, if only I had known this day would come. I would not have been so afraid growing up." She looked down and away, then back to her memories. "I would have been a better mother to my kids! To my poor son!"

Esther stopped her, "No, Laria. No. Don't punish yourself." Her voice softened, "God knows you, Larie," and looked into Candelaria's eyes with Esther's wisdom. "He loves you and He knows that no mother can be perfect." She shook her head in disgust and frustration. "All those people who blame the mothers for their sons becoming all messed-up inside, are forgetting about those sons having a mind of their own and being *responsible* for themselves!"

She emphasized the last she would say on the matter, because Rosa and Coco were walking toward them. Fifty years of life experience were drawn from as she spoke. "Laria, listen to me." She became very serious as she put her arm around Candelaria to comfort her, her voice but a whisper. "God and His angels watch over *all* of us, guiding us all the time, never giving up on us." Candelaria looked into her friend's eyes. Esther continued, "God is carrying Jim *in His arms* now! *He's* in charge. Don't ever forget that."

CHAPTER TWENTY-ONE

The day began in pink and blue. The trees rustled quietly in the shifting breezes. The sky nearly matched the blue of bridesmaids' long, flowing dresses. White corsages adorned their wrists, while white sunhats, shading shy, young faces, waved like kerchief banners to herald the day. A procession of cars arrived at the church, bedecked in pink and white carnations. Shiny and clean, their white sidewalls were spotless, with chrome glistening, all waxed and polished.

Rosa's family led the procession in Rosa's car, repaired for the occasion. They were followed by Buster's family, his parents and his brothers, proud to ride in the new car Buster promised Rosa. A cardboard sign, spray painted with, "Just Married," lay in the trunk, along with milk cartons tied together to drag behind, and Buster's suitcase for the honeymoon paid for by Mr. Goodman.

Patience McGrew directed everyone, the caterers, the florist, the bridesmaids, the groomsmen, even the families. Candelaria thanked her repeatedly. The McGrew's even paid for the tuxedos and dresses, including her own. No one had ever been so generous to her family, or to any family in Edenville and Pine Way, and so graciously, Candelaria did not feel indebted for life, only that it was a special day provided for everyone.

Rosa, when she first saw him on the dance floor, was touched by her brother, Jim, looking so handsome in his tuxedo, taking her hand to dance with her at the reception held at the McGrew's. The song that played, about a brother and sister, he especially requested, he whispered to her. It brought to the forefront, in her thoughts and in her heart, their shared childhood years through the Depression and the war, the pain and suffering, the joyous days, the fun and the laughter.

Rosa listened to the words of the song, while looking into her brother's eyes, and said, "Dad would be so proud of you, Jim."

He embraced her tightly and said, "Thank you, Rosa. Dad would be proud of you, too."

When the music stopped, he let her go, holding her hand lightly in his and admiring her as he said, "You're so beautiful, Rosa. This is your day." He gently released her hand. "I love you," he said, and truly meant it.

The day of Rosa's wedding turned out to be the last time she saw her brother alive. Between being newly married, working, and helping her mother, her life was full. She never forgot what Sylvia told her. Rosa knew from gossip circulating in the beauty parlor, if things were terribly wrong before they spoke, they were much worse as the months passed. She tried not to think about it, because it only hurt, and because she did all she could. Before the wedding, she asked Father Sanchez about it, when she and Buster first talked with him about getting married.

He spoke to the point, "Jim is in God's hands now, Rosa." He refrained from telling her he paid Jim and Beth a visit, talking privately with Jim, to no avail.

Jim told Father Sanchez to his face, in an angry tone, what he intended to do, "I'm not *ever* giving up Sylvia! So, you better just *back* off! I'm gonna divorce Beth and marry Sylvia and, if it displeases your precious church, then I'll *leave it, too!*"

When Father Sanchez saw him at the wedding, he was thunderstruck by how different Jim appeared, like he was another person. Why, he even felt proud of the young man! He knew Rosa invited Sylvia and Forty, so he paid the Sumner's a special visit, privately warning Sylvia about adultery, advising her not to attend Rosa's wedding. Not only would it be in bad taste, which he did not allude to, it would be disrespectful, which is what he did say.

Although Sylvia ignored Father Sanchez's warning, she did visit Father Jovial, whom she always admired. She opened up to him about her long history with men and her wish to change her ways, to stop seeing Jim Hart, and to begin searching for the source of her fears.

Father Jovial recalled the day he baptized Sylvia. He was standing over the baptismal font while her father, Robert Cadwallader, held her. Over the decades of serving Pine Way, then Edenville, it was the greatest pleasure for him to see each family begin and then grow. He especially loved the history of the valley and its origins in Pine Way, an example of what was lost to modernization. Certainly, he could not deny bringing plumbing and electricity to homes was necessary, but he missed the little general store. It was a delight to see his neighbors, his parishioners, and he appreciated the slower pace of life, which allowed time for pleasantries, how-do-you-do's, and news regarding the lives of these mountain-loving people. Now, he lamented, the automobiles went too fast to enjoy the traveling. He especially enjoyed riding in the buggy, the horse's hooves trotting along, and marveling at the sun-dappled shade on a quiet lane through the woods where picnics awaited its citizenry.

In the early days, when he was a young priest, even younger than Father Sanchez, which made him smile, he always attended the Pine Way picnics. They were held in the warming days of spring. The tall, green grass bent and flowed in the wind along the slopes, rippling like ocean waves. Everyone came, spreading blankets and tarps under the scented pines, weighted down with baskets of food. Immediately, their children ran off to play together. He could still remember the activity, the women gathering to commiserate over some long-suffered problem or another, and the young men playing horseshoes. A loud clank could be heard, ringing through the air each time a horseshoe hit the metal stake and landed on the other horseshoes. It was always followed by the cheering of men and their bantering voices. He knew every person by name. The highlight of the picnic was when someone got up to tell what they remembered about something in history, particularly the town's history.

One instance, unfortunately, came to mind during little Sylvia Cadwallader's baptismal ceremony. He was enjoying someone's rendition of the first time they heard the radio, everyone in hysterics over the storyteller's humorous antics. Looking out into the surrounding woods for no special reason, he appreciated the scenery, in admiration of the day. The rush and clatter of the maple trees in the wind thrilled him and, then, so innocently, he caught sight of two people from whom he quickly averted his gaze.

That day, when Sylvia Cadwallader was baptized, was such a day for seeing things in people he wished he had not seen. Her father was in adoration of the baby he held in his arms, wrapped in her soft, little yellow blanket with pink-flowered print, her pink bonnet framing the face of his unusual child. She did not cry, but contentedly gazed. Her mother did not attend the ceremony. They waited until Sylvia was already months old before having her baptized. He inquired on the whereabouts of Sylvia's mother and, was she feeling well?

With his brother and sister-in-law standing nearby as godparents, in witness to more than Sylvia's baptism, Robert Cadwallader replied in the strangest way. It reminded Father Jovial of those two people he regrettably set eyes on, though briefly, only two years before Sylvia was born.

"Oh, Charity's not much interested in this wee little girl," Robert said, adoring his child with the gentlest, most loving smile. He explained further, "They say it's the birthing spell laid on some mothers once the baby's born. They only know the baby as a part of themselves and, once the child's born, they grieve its loss, and look upon the child who's there as not their own." He reassured the tiny baby girl in his arms, "But, I know who you are, don't I? And you know who I am. You're my baby girl and I'm your Poppy. Isn't that so?"

It was right at that moment, when Father Jovial knew who he saw in the woods that day at the picnic. He was unclear as to the identity of the man, but he realized in sudden horror, who the young woman was, none other than Charity Walker, Sylvia's mother and Robert Cadwallader's wife. They only had the one child, because Charity died after giving birth to a second child, a boy he baptized, post mortem.

Father Jovial saw more than he cared during his long service as parish priest of St. Peter's Catholic Church. He presided over Sylvia and Forty Sumner's wedding and saw them at church every Sunday, occasionally catching Sylvia's eye on another man, or that other man's eye on her. Though his heart grew sad at the time, he learned long ago never to condemn a soul. He believed that was a sin. "Judgement is mine, saith the Lord," was not only a biblical passage, it was a remonstrance to all, that to judge one another was to condemn, damn, even to curse. He could never do that, at least not since Dewey Stewart died, the unfortunate young man he wrongly counseled. Each time Sylvia visited, he chose only to feel joy. Concerns were always present, but love and hopefulness prevailed at the knowledge, she came to him of her own free will, and desired, not only to be repentant, but to be *found.*

"Yes," he said, nodding his head. Seated at his favorite, sunlit window in his favorite cushioned chair, he continued, "She is like a lost lamb who yearns for the Shepherd to find her." He peered through the window pane, seeing across the road to the town square, the people of his community busy with their daily doings.

He told himself to visit Charity Cadwallader's grave, even to bring her flowers. "Your daughter's needin' to know you loved her, little Miss," which is what he called her when she first married. She had her father's spirit, although, thankfully, not his more serious, thieving ways.

Justice was the eldest, then came Prosperous, Patience, and Charity. Patience was the only one who remained alive. He wondered if she could be of any help to Sylvia. This idea gave Father Jovial a task he jotted down in his notepad before setting out to fulfill it, rather impulsively, to be sure, but well-intentioned.

Patience agreed to help her niece any way she could. Considering her daughter, Dottie, who had always been cared for and loved, compelled her to reach out to help Dottie's cousin, Sylvia, who did not receive the same, thoughtful care as a child.

Sylvia wanted to go to Rosa's wedding, but she knew Father Sanchez was right, and instead painted her nails and did the ironing. Forty was quietly reading one of his detective magazines. Their home life seemed peaceful and content. In reality, she feared making changes in her life, to "dig up the past," as Father Jovial phrased it. Surprising herself, she noticed she began to see herself in a new way. Taking this new stand, changing her position, or, perspective, she stepped in to who she truly was, a grown woman. From this point of view, she recognized that her mistakes and unhappy memories were part of the past now. Yet unable to see it absolutely clear, she sensed she was exploring the past, to find the answers to her questions, and maybe discover something she long forgot. One scene appeared in her mind, like a doorway opening, through which she was invited to enter.

Forty lounged on the sofa with his finger in his navel, one leg drawn up, the other propped across it with his bare foot twitching and flipping around. Sylvia knew it meant he was so engrossed in what he was reading, he would soon be fast asleep. Her first thought arrived out of habit, to slip out back and see if Jim was at work. Thankfully, for her better interest, she remembered he was at the wedding. He told her Saturday was "definitely out." Setting the iron to cool, she sat on the back steps where she could see the Catholic church bell tower across the field and the orchards behind, deciding to take a chance. She stepped through the imagined doorway and learned something very important about herself.

The scene was of her mother standing at the kitchen sink in her girdle, bra, and stockings. She spilled something on her dress and removed it right there in the kitchen. She began to daub and dab, then rub, then furiously scrub the darn dress, until she worked herself up into such a state of disgust and frustration, she would likely rip it to shreds if she did not cease. She gave up and leaned over the sink, exhausted, elbows on the edge of it, her face in her hands. She lamented bitterly, "I just wish he'd come home."

Sylvia was only a little girl, sitting in the sunlight shining through the open back door upon the linoleum flooring. Her Aunt Justice had given her a doll. She played quietly, holding it like it was her baby, talking and cooing.

Still bent over the sink, arms still resting on the edge, her mother glared back behind her. With her face pinched up in an angry, "I hate the whole damn world," sort of scowl, she shouted at Sylvia, "Why don't you go play outside?!"

It was a tone Sylvia knew well. It meant, "Do what Mommy says or wish you had." But, she was enjoying the sun and her new doll, and replied, "I wanna play right here."

Her mother strode across the kitchen, behaving not altogether unlike a bawdy mistress, and ripped the doll from Sylvia's arms, throwing it out the back door onto the dirt, yelling, "Do what I tell you!"

Sylvia ran to retrieve her doll, then scurried quickly back into the kitchen as her mother was walking toward the sink. Immediately dropping the doll, she began pummeling the backs of her mother's legs and rear end, and kicking her with all her might. She screamed at her mother, "I *hate* you! I *hate* you!"

The neighbors heard the yelling. Tucker Howard Stewart came running to see what was the matter. Her mother was grabbing and shaking her when he stepped into the kitchen. He hurried to intervene, taking Sylvia into his arms and handing her the doll. Carrying her outside, he gave her a hug and a kiss before setting her down on the back steps. He told her, "You be a good little girl and run along now." Scooting her on her way with a light pat on the rear, he added, "Your momma's upset about things and needs you to play outside, okay?"

Sylvia agreed. Though, looking back at the house, she saw him returning to the kitchen.

She could make out her mother's strange expression as he walked slowly toward her, talking low. It was sort of a half-smile she gave, through half-closed eyelids, as she looked toward him before he shut the door behind.

The scene faded and Sylvia realized Forty was in the kitchen, opening and closing cupboards. She never discussed the past with him much, but she had no one else to talk to about a time when he was a neighbor of her family's and may have seen something.

She called out to him, "Forty?"

He came out onto the back porch, "What is it, sweetheart?"

He stood over her, something she never liked, so she stood up and lit a cigarette. Looking out at the fields and the woods, she asked, "Do you remember my mother?"

"Your mother?"

Sylvia never talked about her mother and father with him. Caught off guard, he shared the first thing that popped into his head, "I remember one time your dad brought your mom some flowers. He picked you up and took you into the house with him." He stopped himself at the part where Mr. Stewart hurried out the back door. Innocently, Forty remembered more about that day.

Their other friend, Tucker, said, "See ya later," and waved goodbye to him. Forty lingered out in the street, watching Tucker run up to his mother. She was on her way home from the drugstore, a small parcel in her hand her son offered to carry. She told him, "No, it's my medicine," and refused to answer any more questions. Tucker ran off and Forty followed him.

Ending up at their playhouse, Fort Sumner, Forty sat with his friend and waited, but Tucker said nothing for a long time, hiding his face and brooding. Eventually, he got mad, saying, "No one ever tells me a damn thing!"

Despite Forty's attempt to avoid any unhappiness, it came up anyway. Even though he understood his old friend was also hurting, he no longer wanted to talk about it, especially since he suspected that he and Sylvia were fooling around, like Jim Hart hinted they were doing. So, he quickly changed the subject. "I'm gonna barbecue those steaks you bought." He left her side and went into the kitchen to begin dinner.

Sylvia knew Forty was withholding something from her, but she followed him into the kitchen, withdrew a can of corn from the cupboard and some store-bought dinner rolls from the freezer to put in the oven, when her husband objected.

"No, it's too hot for the oven." Surprising Sylvia, he added impulsively, "Hey! Let's go try the new restaurant up the hill!"

"Sure!"

Sylvia was enjoying the Forty she remembered as a child and hoped it would last.

Everyone else, she imagined, went to Rosa and Buster's wedding reception. Sylvia asked Forty to take the back road out to the highway, up Pine Way Junction. They dressed and readied to depart, soon driving away from the house. Sylvia wore her freshly ironed dress, extra careful of her freshly painted nails, while Forty was in his tan, freshly ironed slacks and a light-blue polo shirt Sylvia bought for his birthday, which he usually wore to work.

They enjoyed a leisurely drive to the restaurant, stopping to get out of the car to enjoy the view across the valley and pointing out which house belonged to whom. They ate a large and satisfying dinner. Two other couples shared the restaurant with them. After a while, with their stomachs full of roasted chicken and baked potatoes, garlic bread, steamed carrots, and salad with Roquefort dressing and croutons, topped off with a mug of root beer, they drove home. The sun set, but it was yet light outside. Noting how peaceful the day turned out, their individual gazes took in the scenery around them.

Sylvia remarked on the tall pine trees lining the roadside, recalling how their bark smelled like vanilla. Smiling, Forty pulled over to the side of the dirt road. They got out of the car to smell a tree trunk. He praised her memory, "You're right, sweetheart. Vanilla." He patted the tree as one would a horse they admired.

Before returning to the car to continue their drive home, Forty turned to once again take in the view. This time, he noticed the natural scenes, like the immense cottonwood trees down along the valley's edge, bordering the stream. So easily affected by wind, the trees were nearly still in the quiet evening, making it possible to hear water splashing in the creek, winding its way over boulders, bubbling in deep tones where it reached a pool.

Sylvia waited for him by the open car door, one hand resting on top. She scanned the valley for signs of the wedding and the reception.

Lingering at the edge of the embankment, Forty propped one foot on a boulder by the roadside. One hand rested on his leg, while his other hand was on his hip. He was carried off by his own memories, remembering the creek being a favorite place to play. Even his father enjoyed the five-minute walk from their house to visit the rambling stream. Mouthing his ever-present cigar while turning over rocks or picking them up to examine them, he told Forty and the other children who joined them, "People say, there used to be gold in this creek." To a boy, this revelation was nothing short of saying there was treasure buried right under their noses.

Feeling himself the man who had no children with whom to share such experiences, the sound of an approaching car suddenly caught his attention. It was a faded red Chevy Corvair, speeding toward them from the direction of Pine Way. He watched as the car got closer, immediately recognizing the young man from the fire crew who put out Ev Mendoza's house fire. Ev's housekeeper was on the passenger's side, gripping the dashboard and looking behind them, then ahead, frantic and wild-eyed. The car sped past, its passengers seemingly unaware Forty intensely watched them from the side of the road.

"Now, what was that all about?"

Sylvia was growing chilled, arms wrapped about her, rubbing her arms. The day may have gotten too warm for cooking, but the nights were yet cool enough for a sweater, she thought. She was oblivious to anything unusual.

They got back into the car and, while driving homeward, the siren from the volunteer fire department sounded across the valley, alerting Forty's investigative nature into action. He pounded the steering wheel and announced, "We gotta get home!"

Sylvia rolled her eyes, knowing Detective Forty was at it again.

CHAPTER TWENTY-TWO

Sylvia paused before getting out of the car. The smoke of a nearby fire had reached their home. The sharp peel of a siren swiftly carried through the woods, drawing near. Soon, the volunteer fire truck came by, turning down Jim and Beth Hart's driveway. Forty transformed into a madman, trying to hurry into the house, tripping over the porch steps and nearly colliding into the front door. Frantically, he tried unlocking it, but dropped his keys. Pounding his fist on the door jamb, a splinter caught in his hand. He cried out in pain and frustration, though he managed to finally open the door and hurry inside, leaving his wife ignored. She hesitantly followed behind in his wake, entering their home and turning on the lamp in their living room. Observing her husband, she felt helpless to stop him, becoming increasingly frightened. He appeared to be in an exceptionally unstable frame of mind.

Forty first wanted to grab his Bible from the coffee table and pray, but thought he should get his gun instead. Leaping and stumbling, he made his way up the darkening stairwell to the useless derringer's hiding place before returning downstairs and running out the front door. Seconds later, he ran back in, having changed his mind, and snatched up his Bible. Reminiscent of his father, he halted before going out the door again, pointing his finger at Sylvia, commanding her to stay in the house.

"Stay *put!* I don't want to come home and find you gone off somewhere!"

He turned and went out the door, slamming it behind. Shook up and alone, Sylvia began to unconsciously pace the floor of their living room where, innocently, the doorway to her childhood opened once more, beckoning her to enter. She did so, though only far enough to see what was being shown to her. It was her mother, Charity Cadwallader, who was also alone, her husband gone off to war. Infrequent letters arrived with money and a few words, which had become meaningless.

"I love you. Hug Sylvia for me."

Charity neglected her little girl, often sent her away to stay with Aunt Justice Walker, who adored Sylvia. Aunt Justice curled her hair and fussed over her, made her clothes, even matching sets for her dolls. Justice wanted this little girl for her own, terribly disappointed in the way her youngest sister treated the darling little thing, which is how she saw her niece.

In Sylvia's memory, she saw her mother growing more anxious, pacing, like Sylvia, herself, was doing. Her mother wore a new dress Aunt Justice made for her. Nearby, stood the unwanted child, watching her mother's every move. Sylvia stopped and fearfully beheld her own dress. Only then, did she begin to see that she had somehow become her mother. This observation struck her hard. Seeing the truth was more difficult than avoiding it.

Holding herself, as if to hold in what wanted so badly to be heard, the tears that begged release ran down her face. She remembered being that small child who needed attention and affection from her mother, though it rarely came.

Her mother told her one night to go next door to the Stewart's and tell them something needed fixing. In her pajamas and slippers, Sylvia peeked out the door. The neighbor's house seemed too far away for an errand in the night, yet, off she ran, falling once and getting up, before timidly knocking on the Stewart's back door. Her friend, Tucker, answered.

"What're you doin' over here? It's late." Glancing at the Cadwallader's house, he assessed the situation, opening the door wider to let her in, saying, "Come on."

He called out to his father. "Dad? Sylvia's here."

Upon seeing her, the eager man instantly tossed aside his newspaper, as if years had dropped from his life and he was young again. He gave a brief hello to her, a pat on the head in passing, and a hasty, "goodbye, I'll be right back," to them both, and was out the door.

She timidly followed Tucker into the boys' bedroom and, together, they looked at picture books, dug through a box of small toys, and played whatever they felt like playing. Dewey shushed them, because he had to get up early to go to work and needed to sleep. Usually, their father returned and carried her home.

"There, there, little one," he would say. "I've gotcha," which somehow always made things better. In his arms, she pretended that Mr. Stewart was her father, hoping for another moment like that again, forgetful of why they took place at all.

Mrs. Stewart had died by that time. Sylvia recalled the children yet living at home. She imagined they knew about the shamefully iniquitous arrangement between their father and her mother. Once, she overheard the girls in their bedroom, talking before going to sleep. It was one of those nights.

"I wish Mother was here," Marjorie said wistfully.

Angrily, Lois remarked, "She's dead, you dope."

"Still...what are we supposed to do? She's married!"

"There's nothing we can do, except move out, soon as we're old enough!"

Standing by the girl's bedroom door, waiting to use the bathroom, Sylvia came to believe that nobody wanted her. She tiptoed to the boy's room and nestled onto a makeshift bed of blankets, like a kitten, and fell asleep. Early in the morning, before sunrise, she returned home. Across the kitchen and living room, into her mother's room, she ever so quietly climbed into bed between Mr. Stewart and her mother, who were soundly sleeping.

• • •

Sylvia stepped off the back porch, recalling her earlier conversation with Forty, in which she asked if he remembered her mother. Regretting having brought it up, she walked away from their home, taking her usual route to get to Jim's workplace. Out the back alleyway, looking around her and back toward the house, she carefully made her way into the dusky night air. The evening song of crickets halted as she passed their chorus ground amidst the weedy roadside. The air held the harsh smell of smoke, hanging like a pall in the woodland growth of trees and vines. Noticing people driving into and out of the neighborhood, she waited in the shadows beyond the reach of Pine Way's one streetlight until they passed. She knew Jim would be at the barn, tending to his horses before checking on his house. She needed to see him and was hoping he needed to see her.

Someone called the McGrew's residence and told them about the fire. Patty's husband, Clarence "Daddy" McGrew, informed the guests at the reception who lived in Pine Way, to hurry home and check on their houses. Jim Hart left without delay, along with several others. Beth picked up her purse and stood up, prepared to go with him, but Jim's mother told her to wait and let Jim take care of things.

The fire was burning through some tall weeds near one corner of Jim and Beth's house. Fortunately, for them, the firefighters controlled the small blaze until they extinguished the flames. While the crews collected the hoses and tools, Forty spotted the young man he saw earlier with Ev Mendoza's old housekeeper. He knew something was wrong. He called aside the captain of the volunteer fire department to inform him what he observed.

"That guy over there. I saw him here another night! And, just this evening, I saw him driving past me with that girl who used to live with Ev Mendoza. They were driving real fast down Pine Way Junction, like they were being chased!"

The captain was exasperated with Forty's meddling, fully prepared to give him a talking-to. "Forty!" He had a grieved expression on his face, had missed his dinner, and would likely return home to a plate of cold meat and soggy bread. He said, "Forty, they live here in Edenville," his open hand striking the air for emphasis. "Of course, you're gonna see them around." He had enough, pointedly jabbing his finger back up the driveway. "Now, why don't you go home and let us do our job. You've done enough. Really. You've done e-nough."

Forty stepped off to the side, determined to watch his suspect. He refused to leave.

Once they drove away, even a guilty man could not take Forty seriously, seeing him standing in the dark like he had missed his bus. With concerns now on other matters ahead, they ignored what the rearview mirrors revealed, Forty's flashlight beam, searching for clues. His worthless gun, laying in the road where it fell, also went unseen.

Meanwhile, Jim stopped at the barn to check on his horses. Shep and Tessie came running up to him from the direction of his house, whining and agitated. The horses whinnied loudly. He unlocked the barn and grabbed the lantern, striking a match with which to light it. He removed his tuxedo jacket and put on his coveralls. Hanging the lantern near the stalls, he tried calming the horses. "It's okay. It's okay," he said. "Fire's not gonna hurt you. Everything's gonna be all right."

Walter Henry and Millie were out of town with Johnny for the weekend. Jim wished his partner was here, not only for his own sake, so he could check on his house, but for the sake of everyone at the wedding, most especially his sister, Rosa. Managing to calm the horses, he stepped out of the barn to walk a ways down the road, to look for any sign of fire. Though he could smell the smoke, he knew the fire was out once he saw the volunteer fire truck approaching. It stopped nearby and the captain rolled down the window. Jim ran to meet him.

"Almost got your house burned down, Jim." The captain shouted over the engine noise, "Fire was right next to it! You need to clear that brush around your house! If we hadn't have gotten there when we had," hooking a thumb through the air in that direction, "your house would've been torched!" He waited for Jim's response.

Jim was shocked. "Thank you, Mr. Andrews! I appreciate it." He reached up to shake the man's hand. "I'll do that! Walter and

I will clear those weeds away!" It was a well-meant promise, though one he would never keep.

The captain started rolling his window back up, but stopped himself. He recalled Forty, left behind at Jim's house. He was unsure whether he should mention it or not, including what Forty reported to him. So, rolling the window down again, he casually said, "Oh, Jim!" Jim waited. The captain chose his words carefully, pushing his loose hardhat further back on his head, before saying, "If you get a chance, come by the station. We need to do an investigation into how that fire might have gotten started." Seeing Jim's face grow concerned and worried, he reassured him, "No big deal. Just paperwork. You know how it is!" He laughed to put Jim at ease. Jim promised to stop by on Monday, while the fire captain made a mental note to send someone he knew over to Jim's house to investigate.

The truck drove off, catching Sylvia in their headlights before she crossed the road. The captain, Richard Andrews, shook his head, but said nothing. He shifted the stubborn old gears and they bounced along in the big fire truck.

Although surprised to see her, it was not long before Jim was leading Sylvia up to the loft. "We don't have much time," he said. He needed to get back to the wedding reception.

"I know," Sylvia said, her voice low. She had to return home to her suspicious husband.

What Sylvia craved in the moment, was to believe that she and Jim were in love, to be young again...and wanted. She fought to suspend the urgings of the past, to instead encapsulate a lost dream, shield it from her troubles and from Jim's. But, change was due to come. Her innocence was lost, as was his, and the truth, she would soon learn, enlightens even those who seek to dwell in the dark.

Watching Jim hastily spread the blanket upon the hay, a thought came to her, more like a tender knowing. The lantern light shone faintly from below, illuminating his features in golden light and shadow. His back, broad and strong, attracted her to him, and she drew her hand across it, laying her head on his shoulder. Drawing away, she caught the look on his face exposing his childlike worry, as though he was afraid, having become that young, teenaged boy whom she remembered well.

CHAPTER TWENTY-THREE

In the Edenville town square, Johnny Henry walked along the street, looking far ahead at some terrible, imagined scene. His orange, white, and green striped t-shirt had become too small for him, his Keds worn, with undone laces flapping around, and his jeans faded and in rags. Holes and ripped areas in the cloth allowed the air to blow through, but his mind was not on his clothes. School was out for the day, and it was hot, that drippy, sweaty kind of heat where you fear there may not be enough air to breathe, it feels so close and stifling. But, the look of worry on his face had nothing to do with the weather. It had everything to do with Jim. Johnny needed to see him, his day filled with worry for his friend, the man he loved and admired.

School children left in buses or waited along the curb for their parents. Many of them walked down the sidewalk to stop by the drugstore for candy. A few of the other kids filed ahead of Johnny into Millie's Kitchen for ice cream, one boy pushing him aside. Under his breath, he said to Johnny, "Out of the way, Squirt!" Soon, the fretful boy had his own dish of Neapolitan placed before him, anxious, pestering Walter Henry about when they might leave for the barn.

Walter Henry was smiling and Millie was laughing over a joke she told him. A pencil behind her ear and a pad upon which to write customer's orders were at the ready for the early evening diners. Her blue and white, starched and pressed uniform was splattered with grease from the lunch crowd, her feet aching in her expensive white shoes, which the school nurse also wore, according to Johnny. It was time for them to get back to work, so they said their goodbyes. Millie noticed Johnny's ice cream sat untouched in the small dish, though dismissed it in her rush to get busy.

Commenting on how hot the day was turning out, Walter Henry and the boy left for the blacksmith shop and livery stable. A sheriff's car drove past on Edenville Drive, going toward Pine Way. At the sight of it, Johnny grew more anxious, urging Walter Henry to hurry, which the old man refused to do.

"Calm down," he said.

Minutes later, they arrived at the barn. Johnny flung the truck door open and jumped out, running into the building, but Jim was nowhere to be found. He pleaded with Walter Henry, "Couldn't I just go and see if maybe Jim's home?"

"No," the man said. "Leave him be." Though, seeing Johnny's downcast face as they set to work, Walter Henry gently added, "He's probably out somewhere, anyway."

They were not the only ones who saw the sheriff's car. Candelaria noticed it when she walked past the diner on her way home from the school. She pulled the strap of her purse higher onto her shoulder and repositioned the notebooks in her arms. Feeling the sun beating down on her and perspiration breaking out beneath her clothes, she looked forward to the shade at her house. She debated whether to walk straight over to Rosa and Buster's house on Magnolia Lane. Rosa invited her to dinner, adding that she had some special news for everyone. Buster's parents were also invited. It was yet early, and Candelaria preferred to freshen up and change into some cooler clothes, so she decided to go home.

She was not surprised about Rosa's news, coming nearly a year after the wedding. Well, she had news of her own, and no one else with whom to share it, other than her daughter, except the school librarian. Miss Winters devoted many long hours and late evenings helping her with her writing. Getting to know the younger woman, she wished her son had married someone like Miss Winters. Although, she regretted being so bold as to mention it. Afterward, she reminded herself never to repeat her son's name to that woman.

Straightening her papers before she left the library, placing all of her work in a notebook, and picking up her purse, Candelaria readied to go home, when Miss Winters breezed into her office.

"All done for the day?"

"Yes, thank you."

"Have you heard anything about your last article? Any fans seeking you out?" Miss Winters' excitement, while not boisterous, was nonetheless infectious.

Candelaria laughed lightly. "No, but I'm hopeful it got positive reviews."

They walked to the door together, continuing their small talk.

Miss Winters inquired, "You're off to your daughter's for dinner?"

"Yes. Keeping my fingers crossed about the news."

"Oh? What news?" Miss Winters was happily intrigued.

Placing her hand on the doorknob and turning it, Candelaria shared, "I'm hoping it's about a baby on the way." She pushed against the door, and it opened.

"Well...it could be." The librarian followed Candelaria outside and locked the door while inquiring further, "How long have they been married?"

"Umm...almost a year."

"Ooo! A baby, it is!"

They laughed outright by this time, standing together in front of the library for a few more minutes. The librarian feigned lamenting about marriage and raising children not being in her stars. It was merely her fate to grow old, she said, surrounded by children she could not take home and handsome teachers she could not marry.

Candelaria then said, "I wish my son married someone like you. You're a very kind and warm-hearted person, Miss Winters. I dread going to my daughter's tonight simply because *she* will be there." She meant Beth, because she heard Rosa also invited her and Jim. Although, she dreaded seeing her son. She dwelled on this momentarily, regretting saying what she had to the librarian, only half-listening to her response.

"Well, I was a very different person when I was young. You may not have wanted him to marry me then and, now, I very much doubt he has any interest in a boring school librarian, like some old spinster lady." She added under her breath, "at least that's my impression."

When Candelaria arrived at home, she recalled the librarian's words, wondering if Miss Winters ever met her son. She said aloud to herself, "Hmph. That woman's got to be *years* older than Jim!"

After a while, when Rosa stopped by to pick her up, Candelaria immediately asked her daughter, "So, what's the news, Rosa?"

"No, Mom, you're just going to have to wait like everyone else." Rosa was not about to spoil the surprise, yet her mother would not relent.

"Is it a baby? Tell me!" Candelaria was thrilled at the idea.

Traveling along Edenville Drive toward Magnolia Lane, a second sheriff's car drove past, as well as a coroner's car, a truck, and an unmarked vehicle, heading in the direction of Pine Way. Rosa was too busy fending off her mother's questioning to notice. Candelaria was excited. Imagining what it would be like to hold a baby in her arms again, brought her joy. Though, her own news was cause for celebration.

To everyone at the elementary school, Candelaria was simply, "Mrs. Hart." An English teacher for the older students learned she wrote stories and articles using the librarian's typewriter. He became inspired by Mrs. Hart's dedication, and curious. After reading an article by a Candelaria Mendoza, which included a picture of her, he happily discovered they were the same person. Excited to have such a writer in their own town, he tried to meet her, and finally did that very afternoon.

"Mrs. Hart?"

He hurried to catch up to her before she left the school grounds. She had her short hair done earlier in a soft perm, wore a royal blue, cotton dress with cuffed short sleeves, a belt, and blue clip-on earrings. He readily introduced himself and asked if they could talk, to which she agreed. Sitting on the curb in front of the school together, in the sweltering heat, the teacher began sharing his ideas and concerns. His hands went from clasping then flying out again, while he excitedly talked to her. Too uncomfortable in the hot sun, Candelaria stood up and dusted off her dress, squinting and shading her eyes as she continued listening to him.

Unaware of her discomfort, he said, "When I read your article in *People's Awareness, Growth, and Enlightenment* magazine, I was so impressed with your knowledge of the issues facing us today *and* with your writing talent."

He wore gray slacks, a light-blue, short-sleeved shirt, and a gray tie, along with wingtip shoes. His youthful enthusiasm overwhelmed Candelaria's more reserved nature. She noticed that his blondish brown hair was longer than most men in their town wore their hair. It swept down into his face. Every so often, he would comb it back with his fingers or merely whip it back into place with a jerk of his head.

Wanting to be on her way, she said, "Thank you, for telling me. I'm glad somebody likes what I've written."

"Oh, it was superb! PAGE is a top publication, very prestigious. To be published by them, simply means . . ." He searched for the words, then exclaimed, "You've arrived!"

Candelaria was taken aback, about to say, "Arrived where?" It dawned on her he meant she was good. "Well, thank you. I'm pleased," and now very much ready to gather her things and go home.

He asked her if she would be willing to speak at the next Parent-Teacher Advisory Group meeting, calling it, "P-TAG." He wanted to encourage creative writing in the local schools, perhaps even form a writer's group or a class for people in the evenings. One of his ideas was to bring more activities to their schools and community, offering more than farming or building suitcases.

Candelaria could not hear him anymore, about ready to faint from the heat, her notebooks heavy and cumbersome. He was an intelligent man, used to talking a lot to his students who had no choice but to listen, she imagined. She politely answered, "I'll have to think about it," which he was pleased to hear, shaking her hand as he stood up, almost knocking her off the curb.

"Could you wait just a minute? I have something I'd like you to— It'll just take a minute." He put his hand out as he spoke, to motion to her to wait. He practically ran back to his classroom, unlocked the door, then quickly went in, slid across the floor, and, barely out of breath, grabbed something before returning to Candelaria. He combed his hair back with his fingers, then showed her the magazine in which her article had been published. He asked, "Do you think you could autograph this for me?"

He complimented her again about the article, adding that it spoke more to young people, especially college students. Candelaria was not able to appreciate it at the time, quickly signing her name where he pointed, so she could say goodbye and go home. After she made her escape, she breathed a sigh of relief and wondered if he was one of the handsome young teachers to whom Miss Winters had referred.

During dinner at Rosa's, they missed the coroner's team and its entourage leaving Edenville. After dinner, Candelaria was relieved her son and his wife had not come. Rosa took her home, then followed her into the farmworker's shack. They were quiet, almost somber, Candelaria having mixed feelings about Rosa's news. She left the front door open and latched the screen door, walking around the small house to open the few windows to catch a breeze.

Disappointed in her mother, Rosa pouted as she followed behind. "Buster thinks I'd make a great teacher, Mom." She crossed her arms in front of her. "I thought you'd be happy...pleased. You always worked."

Candelaria was too tired to be defensive. She worked long hours in the orchards and was trying to keep up her writing, which only paid in copies of magazines, until her most recent article the teacher read. A check came in the mail, her first payment. This was the news she wanted to share with Rosa. She could earn money doing what she loved. Her sense of having "arrived" had only this practical meaning to her, not the status or reputable one the teacher implied. Whether his praise matched the supposed prestige of her being published in this particular magazine, was of no consequence to her. Although, Rosa's news surprised even Buster's parents. What about children?

Candelaria apologized, "I'm sorry, Rosa." She confessed to her daughter, "I had expected baby news. What mother wouldn't?"

Rosa refused to let it go. "Buster and I are still going to have kids." But, her mother said nothing. She wondered if something was bothering her. "Mom? Are you okay?"

"Oh, Rosa, I don't know. It's probably just the heat." Candelaria took off her earrings, slipped off her high heels, and sauntered into the bedroom.

Rosa disliked having to pry an explanation out of her. She needed to get home to her husband. "Here we go," she commented in frustration, unable to leave while her mother was behaving so depressed. The usual expression of sorrow on her mother's face had become more pronounced, which concerned Rosa. She decided to press the matter. "What's going on, Mom?" It came out a bit stern, but Rosa was not in the mood for what she saw as her mother's stall tactics and avoidance games.

"I can't talk about it."

Candelaria took off her dress and put on a thin robe. She sat quietly with Rosa in the living room. Sweat ran down the backs of her legs even while sitting still. She asked Rosa to get them both some ice water.

Rosa concluded that her mother's state of mind probably had nothing to do with her news about studying to become a teacher. She figured it had everything to do with something neither of them talked about anymore. "It's Jim, isn't it? Did you see him?"

Candelaria saw him only two days before and vowed never to try talking to him again. Any further contact had to come from him and only him. Rosa tried to draw it out of her, but Candelaria really did not care to discuss it, or even think about it.

Rosa felt bad. "I'm sorry, Mom." Ready to let the whole matter go, she got up from the sofa. "I need to get home." She hugged and kissed her mother before going into the kitchen.

On her way out the door, she saw a check sitting on the table. Glancing at the signatory and the name of the publisher, she started to ask her mother about it, but stopped herself. Leaving her mother alone, and obviously upset about something, made Rosa feel guilty. To cope, she merely told herself that her mom would be okay once she rested. Taking the guilt parked on her shoulders, she dumped it off the side of the road and drove home in her Buick Starlight.

When she arrived at her house, she happened to see Walter Henry and Johnny in town. It appeared they were arguing about something in front of the diner, so she waited, watching them. Millie came out of the diner and Johnny hurried to her, crying loudly as she held him in her arms. Concerned for the boy, Rosa wondered what could have happened. Tearing herself away, she walked across the lawn to go into the house. It was not long before the telephone rang, the news arriving that she and her mother had feared for a very long time.

CHAPTER TWENTY-FOUR

After Rosa left her house, Candelaria reminisced about her husband. Jimmy Hart was a handsome man, she recalled, with light-brown hair he kept neatly trimmed, though he never cared for "greasing it up," as he used to say. An aquiline nose and amber-colored eyes suited his ever-present smile. His body was compact and he always wore blue jeans, a denim jacket, cowboy boots, and a cowboy hat. He never wanted to attend the rodeo held every year at the county fairgrounds. Being renowned or flashy never interested him. Like a worker bee, he busily went about his day, quietly humming to himself. He loved being outdoors, close to the land and the way he lived upon it, amongst good people and, always, the horses. Though he was offered higher-paying jobs elsewhere, he apparently had no desire to leave Pine Way, because they never moved.

The sun never felt so warm, nor the breeze so cool as the moment Candelaria Mendoza set eyes on him. Her father's family wanted her to have a horse for her own as a high school graduation gift. Her great-uncle, Dexter Shows-His-Guns, talked her parents into seeing one for sale at the livery stable. Herman

Mendoza, her father's younger brother, stepped out of the newspaper office to greet them. Even her Grandma Lucy Shoseegan, Dexter's sister, joined in the fun that day. They were delighted when a beautiful, very dainty and tiny-hoofed, bay mare, whinnied to her from its stall. Everyone agreed, Castanets was the horse for her.

Each family member pitched in to help pay for it. Their Candelaria had done well in school and deserved the gift, Grandma Lucy was sure to stress. It came with a hand-crafted, western saddle and an old, green, pink, and white, Mexican-style saddle blanket. Uncle Dexter helped her mount the horse and off it trotted, out of the barn and into the sun, the snappy sound of its quick-paced trot lending just reason for its name.

Jimmy came walking up the path from his parent's house and caught sight of her, a young woman with long, black hair drawn up into a pony tail. She remembered him telling her later that he instantly admired what, to him, was the prettiest sight in all the world. He told her he knew she was the girl he would marry, that he could almost see the dream she carried, riding up and down the road, her family cheering.

It was a good day, a family day, a day of possibilities. The children came, first Rosa, then Jim and, later, the two they buried before anyone even got to know them. Yet, their life was full, it seemed, complete. They had enough money, their own house, and were partners with Walter Henry in their own—

Remaining seated on the sofa facing her television, Candelaria drifted further along in her remembrances, staring blankly into space. Rosa's departure hardly registered in her awareness. A vision of a lion formulated in her imagination, padding heavily, yet gracefully toward her. Accompanying it, another vision so clear, of her husband, came to her and then faded. She wanted to run after him, to call him back! Oh, how she missed him! The lion turned and walked away, as though summoning her, which she promptly heeded, too tired and distraught to fight it. Giving up, she lay down.

She remembered seeing Jim with Shep one time, experiencing a faint sense about her son, and herself. A long day at work in the orchards lay behind her. She walked past Goodman's Hardware Store on the way home, carrying her lunch pail and thermos. She noticed Jim standing beside his truck petting Shep, who always rode in the truck bed. People walked past her son, darting glances and commenting to one another, ignoring him. For some reason, that brief scene reminded her of something as innocuous as the cover of *The Saturday Evening Post*, and yet so damning, because of what it represented to her. It portrayed an America in which neither she nor her son would ever be a part, solely because their skin was brown. Life, that day, suddenly felt very unfair. Her muddy work clothes, her hair in a tattered bandanna bonnet stood out, along with the dusty road she traveled homeward. She felt as dirty and worn, and as forgotten, as the old road leading to Pine Way.

In her tiresome grief, Candelaria could only weep, mad at God, fearing that Jim would never get the chance to be anything more than a problem child who grew up to become another angry, broken man. Though, what truly frightened her, was an incident that took place only two days ago. It was the day she wanted very much to forget, which Rosa attempted to pry from her. Returning to her in a lion's gaze, it arrived in her memory, as though adrift on the wind that blew somewhere far off, somewhere . . .

• • •

The little shacks in Villa Boracho could not keep any secrets to themselves when last she saw her son. All was laid bare for the eyes and ears of its residents. When Jim showed up, riding a horse and wearing his father's cowboy hat, Candelaria believed it was his father's ghost. She heard the bright, clippety-clippety trotting of a horse and hurried out onto the porch to see. Her heart shook and shuddered, the tears of its sudden leap into her throat halted, calling to him, almost saying, "Jimmy!" But, she said, "Jim! Look at you! What a beautiful horse!" She was stunned by how much he resembled his father. She ran down the steps and over to him. Like a dream it was, like all other life faded away, and they were the only two people in the world.

"Oh, it's such a pretty horse, Jim! Whose is it?"

"I'm gonna buy it for Johnny." He sounded so confident.

She reproached herself for doubting him, petting the horse's neck, talking sweetly to it. He kept saying something about Johnny, how the boy needed a horse, and how well he took care of them. She paid little attention to what he said, namely some plans he made regarding the boy. What got through to her was, "Rosa's gonna have kids. They'll need a horse to ride, too. This one's perfect, so gentle." Candelaria agreed, her face beaming with the joy she felt within herself. Jim was happy by all appearances.

"Come on and ride it, Mom." Dismounting the horse and handing her the reins, he said, "Come on. You used to ride." He was very pleased with himself.

She was overwhelmed. He was so much like his father! Yes, she used to ride, but that was before her husband was killed by a horse. Her heart, her whole inner being seemed to quiver from a mixture of joy and terror. A full day of work in the orchards was over. She needed to change out of her dirty and wet clothes. The thrift store work boots she wore, their ragged laces only long enough to tie partway, were caked in mud. She was planning to clean up and have lunch, then walk to the school to use the typewriter. Nevertheless, she agreed.

"Okay, but slowly."

She put her foot in the stirrup and swung herself into the saddle. So easy and natural, she directed the horse and it turned around, walking along the road, with Jim walking beside her.

Esther was watching from her kitchen window. Shouting as quietly as she could, she called to her husband, "Hey, *Jorge!*"

He entered the kitchen, seeing his wife rapidly fanning her hand, urging him to come to the window. He was scratching his backside, and elsewhere, his undershirt dirty and sweaty from working in the orchards, and asked, "Isn't that Little Jimmy?" Peering out the window, he yawned, then went back to his nap on the couch.

Esther was displeased with his lack of interest and followed him with her scornful glare. "You don't know anything!" She heard him grunt. "This is a good sign." She went back to her observing. Her husband mumbled something, which sounded like, "mind your own business," so she went outside to escape his criticism.

Watching the two going toward Pine Way, something caught her eye, startling her. It was Sylvia Sumner, coming down the alleyway behind the houses across the road, walking toward the barn. "Uh, oh!" Esther could barely stand to watch anymore. "Someone oughta knock that silly woman into the weeds!" Nevertheless, she kept following the progress of each, relieved when Jim and her friend kept walking. She went back inside to report it all to her snoozing husband.

At the barn, Candelaria dismounted the horse, feeling uncomfortable after seeing Sylvia. Nothing had changed with Jim, after all, she cynically concluded. That woman was on her way to meet him and he pretended not to notice, of this she was certain. She decided it was best to go home before she said something she would later regret. Before she did so, Jim's dog,

Tessie, ran to her, puppies yapping from one of the stalls. Jim took the horse from her. She pet the dog, looking across the barn at two whimpering puppies frantically trying to climb out of the stall. She was unaware of the expression on her face, her mouth pinched, her jaw set. Instead of saying to Jim, "goodbye, thank you," and walking away, she stubbornly followed him further into the barn.

Immediately, she felt something pressing on her conscience, urging her to stop and go home, back to her life beginning to flower after all her careful tending. Was it God? She wondered, wanting Him to leave her be, so she could do what she so yearned to do, to talk openly with Jim about his problems. While he softly praised the horse and removed the saddle and bridle, a struggle ensued within her. Determined to have her way, she said it, what she would regret the rest of her life, the words she could not make unsaid.

"What's happened to you, Jim? Why have you become so—"

Suddenly, a light sifting of dust and fine bits of straw drifted from the loft above, and Candelaria froze, aghast by what she saw. Sylvia?! Candelaria feared it was true.

Rapidly losing control, a whole string of names came to her that she wanted to yell at that woman, hiding directly above them, she believed. She imagined pulling her down, beating and kicking her and— She imagined running away, fleeing that place of sin and degradation so fast, the wind from her swiftly moving legs would cleanse it from her! How her son behaved so innocently!

Jim had seen Sylvia coming down the road. Earlier, she telephoned, saying she needed to talk to him. Something important came up that worried her terribly, she said. Jim told her to stay away. She pleaded with him over the phone, but he no longer wanted to be the one to whom she could turn, so he hung up and tried to put it out of his mind, though failed. Now, his own anger began to stir. A shadow, always present at his side, crept nearer to him and, in a low voice, he said to his mother, "You want to know?" He turned to face her. She stood several feet away from him, wearing his father's old dungarees and flannel shirt. Wrung out and worn down, he discerned, and only seeing the worst in him, as usual. He turned away. The shadow subsided momentarily, waiting.

Candelaria was unable to refrain from saying what she would later regret most of all, "I'm sorry, Jim, for whatever happened, but your father and I loved you. We adored you! Whatever is going on, between you and that woman— That is all *your* doing!"

Regret for all the years he remained in that town, instead of going away to college, infiltrated Jim's heart. Tiresome complaints of past wrongdoings came alive in that moment, like an all-out assault. Underneath his shirt sleeves, the scars on his forearms, from his self-hating artwork, began to burn, so he squeezed and gripped them, trying to rub out the pain. Unexpectedly, his buried feelings toward his mother, rose to the surface unchecked.

"You never let me decide for my*self!*"

He yanked off his gloves and tossed them onto a barrel lid, purposefully striding across the barn to shout at her, "You never really saw me! You don't see me now!" And it came pouring out, "All you see is *Dad!*" His tears came in his release of the torment he harbored within himself. "Well, I'm not him!" By then, Jim could not stop himself from saying, "You even gave me his name!" With one hand he swept the air into a fist and a finger pointing toward the door, as he commanded her, stabbing the air, "Why don't you just go home and *leave me alone!*"

Automatically and gladly, Candelaria left, like a scolded child, moving without knowing it was she who moved. Once out of sight of the barn, she ran.

• • •

Peering between the boards from their hiding place in the loft, it was Johnny Henry, not Sylvia Sumner, who watched Candelaria swiftly depart. Below, Jim dropped to his knees, hunched over and sobbing loudly. Hurriedly, the boy climbed down the ladder, soon placing his arms around the man.

"I'll go get my dad, Jim!"

No need for that. Walter Henry ran into the barn, having waited by the door. He had come in search of the boy, but heard the argument between Jim and his mother, so waited outside.

Calmly, he said, "Go and wait in the truck, son."

Jim was sorely in need of some help, he could see, feeling the pain of one day long ago, no doubt.

Carefully approaching his friend, pulling him up and dusting him off, he held him until Jim calmed down, then said, "I've got something I want to show you." He locked up the barn and drove them to his sister's retreat center, so Jim could rest. Millie told him to take Jim to see Sister Ruth. Because of his wife's gentle encouragement, Walter Henry agreed.

Echoes resounded in the closed barn after their departure. The year, 1952. Jim and his father were arguing. His father wanted him to take over the business when he retired, and Jim said, "no," a word he never said to his father.

"What did you say?"

"I said, 'no', that's what I said!" Jim faced his father and went on, "Maybe I've got plans of my own!"

"Oh, yeah? Like what?" His father stood there, hands on hips, waiting to hear Jim's answer.

"I'm gonna go to college."

"College?! You don't want to go to college anymore'n I do!"

Jim got his temper worked up, saying, "I don't want to be like you and live in this *pit!* This *hick* town!"

"Just where you plannin' on livin', son?!"

"I don't care! As long as it's not *here!*"

Candelaria watched her husband when he came home, seeing in his eyes the hurting when their son left the house immediately afterward. She guessed they fought again, placing her hand on his back to console him. "He's just at that age. He'll come around." But, there was no time.

Graduation came and went, and the life any of them thought was awaiting them, stopped in its tracks, dropping dead, as if someone shot it down. The sun never stopped shining and the moon never ceased to wax and to wane, but life had changed for good. 1952 was a year not easily forgotten.

• • •

Sister Ruth came down the path from the spring-fed pond, smiling peacefully. Walter Henry told Johnny to come with him to their cabin, but he refused to cooperate.

"No! I'm gonna stay with Jim!"

Walter Henry firmly grabbed hold of the boy's arm and left Jim's side.

"Hello." Sister Ruth gently greeted Jim. He avoided her gaze and said nothing. In silence, she led him up the mountain.

Walter Henry watched them from a window in his cabin. The pine trees grew so tall, she and Jim appeared like miniature human figures within a grand scene. He knew they were going to the healing place, two large stones beneath the trees, overlooking Pine Valley. He could imagine his sister singing, like music emanating from the heated, sunny air, he remembered well. Would Jim see what Walter Henry, himself, had once seen? Last time he went there, a kindly man came to help him. That was a long time ago, when he was a boy. Lulabelle told him she saw him, too, said it was Jesus. But, Walter Henry yet wondered. What if it was?

"Well, I'm not about to tell anybody," muttered the old man. "They might think I'm some kinda kook."

Unable to bear standing by as his friend and partner underwent the healing he knew his sister was administering, Walter Henry left his cabin. Placing Johnny under Millie's watchful eye, he drove his truck back to the blacksmith shop. In the cooling evening, the light beginning to fade as night approached, he tended the forge with renewed purpose. His right hand pulled down on the handle to the bellows above, the air blowing into the coals, brightening their glow momentarily. It shown upon his face, his eyes alight with it, his leather-aproned form transfixed upon it, and he set to work.

Taking a square rod of iron, he placed it into the hottest part of the coals, remembering Jim's drunken, Mean Uncle Jackson, and the day one small boy was marked by that terrible man. Walter Henry bore witness to Jim's suffering ever since.

The dark of night slowly enveloped the nearly open-air shop. The old man drew the reddened iron from the coals and, placing it upon the anvil, began tapping it with his hammer, changing its shape, creating something new. His sister, Lulabelle, sang up on the mountain, as the young man she watched over, rode down the demons relentlessly stalking him. And Walter Henry danced about the blacksmith's forge, wounded healers, all, never knowing of their shared connection.

CHAPTER TWENTY-FIVE

A solemn figure in black, she appeared, her sorrowful features hidden beneath a lace veil. Candelaria Hart led the procession of mourners across the cemetery lawn. Her son's coffin carried ahead of her by Walter Henry, men from Villa Boracho, and his uncles, weighed upon her shoulders. She sat on a bench provided, along with Rosa and her husband, Buster. Beth sat alone, withdrawn and silent. On a bench next to the church, sat Miss Winters, unnoticed. Jim's coffin rested above the open grave, its true import yet to be revealed.

Candelaria thanked God for Rosa, and for Buster, so kind to her, and for a new baby coming into their lives. Their news brought joy to this sad occasion. Though Sylvia attended Jim's funeral, Candelaria feeling Buster's hand gently gripping her own, she was thankful when the woman left before Jim's burial.

A light breeze blew, cooling the warm day. Coughs and sniffles were heard, and some talked quietly amongst themselves. Others filed slowly to the graveside, followed by Father Sanchez. Rosa drew a large scrapbook out of a bag. It was something she kept for years of their family, most especially of her brother and his high school football career. She gave it to her mother. Upon lifting her veil, Candelaria reacted with astonishment, as though she was given a precious gift.

Straining to keep her voice quiet, she asked her daughter, "*Where did you get this?!*"

"I've been keeping it for years. Just a hobby."

"Oh, Rosa!" Candelaria wrapped her arms around her daughter. "Thank you! Thank you!" She turned the pages of the scrapbook to see newspaper clippings, articles, photos, including an essay Jim wrote in his sophomore year of high school. Alongside it, was an old photograph of a dog they once owned.

The priest began giving his final words and blessing. Not paying attention, Candelaria instead read Jim's essay. Nothing less than a revelation to her, his story told about the dog they had when he and Rosa were kids, named Curly. It was a present from his Uncle Dexter Shows-His-Guns. Long ago, the story went, Dexter's dog, Matilda, had three puppies he gave to Jim and his cousins. Jim wrote in his story they agreed to name them, Larry, Moe, and Curly, which Candelaria doubted—or, was it true? Smoothing the page, she studied the picture of Curly standing on the porch of their house next to Jim, only a young boy. She remembered taking the picture, herself.

She searched her memory for a sign that Jim would attempt to take his own life, only to be faced with guilt and regret. Though he had been in need of help for a very long time, help she finally admitted she could not give him, she was ashamed of her behavior when last she saw him. She needed desperately to love the boy in the photographs, forever smiling her way, scruffy hair and missing teeth in Little League baseball, standing with his teammates on picture day during football season in high school, and his arm around Beth on prom night his senior year.

Her lips barely moving, she asked herself, "Who was he?" Hardly making a sound, she answered in stubborn defiance, "He was the boy who was forced to leave his childhood behind with no father to help guide him into manhood. That's who he was...who he became." Yet, as incense burned and holy water sprinkled his coffin, Candelaria was caught up for a second, knowing he had become a man in his own way.

Previously silent, Beth started to cry. Rosa got up to place her arms around her widowed sister-in-law. Candelaria remained captive by her need for understanding. Everything else took place in a blurry background of images. Jim was right, she finally admitted to herself. She never saw him, only her need for him to be an easier child, one not plagued with problems. She wanted her husband to be alive, and was angry that he was not, which greatly hurt her son.

Her gaze lifted out of her thoughts, removed from the scrapbook and its stories. Closing it and placing it into the bag, she noticed Jim's football medal, laid upon the coffin, now lowering into the grave below. Its ribbon displayed the school colors of yellow, white, and lime green.

Johnny spoke quietly to his father. "He's the town hero, isn't he, Dad?"

Walter Henry replied in a low voice, "Yes, son, he's our hero."

Candelaria's heart could not help but break, the crack from its pain ringing like a stabbing jolt to her breast.

Johnny and Walter Henry's private conversation resumed. "I'm glad they let me put it on his coffin, so he'll have it with him always," Johnny said.

Walter Henry agreed. "I'm glad they did, too."

Candelaria weeped without reservation, unconscious of Buster's arm around her, being drawn in close by his thoughtful embrace.

●　　●　　●

Rosa never gave the medal and Grandma's Little Brag Book to Jim that night he cried in her arms at the livery stable. She decided to give them to her mother. In the end, feeling sorry for Johnny, she returned them to him.

Johnny no longer needed the medal. It sat in the box of once-cherished relics, forgotten, until Millie and Walter Henry married. She wanted to know what was in the box, so Johnny shared it with her.

Even though she remembered the trying incident with Jim's medal, Millie remarked, "Well, that's real nice of Rosa and Jim to let you have this, Johnny." She hugged him.

He no longer cared to hold on to it, though, and decided to give it to someone else. The idea came to him, "I'll give it to someone who's my hero." At first, he thought about his dad, but after Jim's death, he remembered Jim was his hero. Walter Henry took him in and gave him a home, but it was Jim Hart who gave him hope and self-respect. Because of Jim, he had a place in the world at the old, out-of-the-way barn the rest of the world left behind.

When Johnny was a little boy of four or five, Jim lifted him up, so he could pet one of the horses, and told him, "I wish you were my boy," and hugged Johnny close in his arms. He said, "I love you. You're a good boy, Johnny. Don't ever forget that."

•   •   •

Candelaria's notebook and pencil remained placed where she set them on the steps of her little house. While funeral guests gathered at her daughter's, she walked toward Pine Way. The sun lowered in the sky, the day cooling, and the approaching evening hinted of peace. When she reached the brick buildings of the old town, she spotted Walter Henry in the barn. Shyly approaching him, she made sure to express her gratitude for helping at the funeral. Stepping closer, to stand within the sheltering structure, she noticed, for the first time, how different it looked inside compared to when her husband was alive. Supplies, tools, tack, everything neatly organized, showed Jim's careful attention.

Embarrassed, at first, wondering if Walter Henry overheard the argument she had with Jim, she watched him getting ready to feed their lone horse, the very same one she rode that day. Softly speaking her fears, she said, "I'm ashamed, Walt. The last thing I said to Jim—"

"Never you mind about that," Walter Henry said, interrupting her. "It couldn't be helped. Shoot! I'd have probably done the same thing."

The old man had his own guilt with which to contend, including his failed attempt at shielding Johnny from Jim's problems. He, too, recalled that day, when he spotted Sylvia behind the barn. He stopped to yell at her from his truck window, "You git on home, hear me?! Leave that man *alone!*" He continued on his way, seeing her in hasty retreat through his rearview mirror.

Changing the subject, Candelaria asked, "What will happen to the business, Walt?"

Walter Henry swung some alfalfa hay into the horse's stall, gave it some oats and clean water, as the light in the barn grew dim. "Oh...it'll do all right." Petting the horse, he talked gently to it, "That's it, eat up." To Candelaria, he added, "As a matter of fact, Jim——" and faltered a moment "——left everything he owned to Johnny, even this horse, here."

Candelaria was stunned and had no idea what to say.

He said, "Beth's the one I don't know what to do about," and winced like he'd rather pull a tooth than be confronted by another angry woman. Stepping outside, with Candelaria timidly following behind, he stated plainly, "She never cared about the business." Scratching an imaginary itch on his elbow, he glanced at Candelaria and made sure to add, "She cared about Jim." Giving a nod in affirmation, he looked at her. "That much I know."

"What happened? To Jim. Why did he do it?"

It pained Walter Henry to see her so sorrowful, and him, too. It was what he asked himself, "Why do some people rise, while some just keep on falling?" What he said to Candelaria, though, was, "I don't know. I keep going back to that one day here," nodding back toward the inside of the barn. He breathed in deeply and blew it out. "That damn——" He scuffed the bottom of his boot along the dirt a bit, then looked around.

Crickets in the field sang their chirping stridulations. Leaves of elm and alder stirred in rustling drafts of air blowing across the valley. Quiet came the evening's change of guard while, far away and out of reach, the noisy city life sat poised for the coming storm of decades yet to come. No longer shielded from the tumult pressing into their lives, both persistent and unforgiving, Walter Henry and Candelaria yet remained standing in the dusk of an era, neither understanding the changing tide of the restless, fervent world rising up around them. Old and forgotten, it may seem Walter Henry's day was slipping fast, but he still had words to share. He yet had his story to tell, days long gone, though living in everything he witnessed and felt in Pine Way.

"I guess some people have a harder time of it than others," a fitting explanation, he thought. Not able to speak of it again, he turned swiftly on his heels, scraping the dry dirt and grit beneath his boots. Locking up the barn, he said, "You take care now." Nodding his head to say "good night" to her, he walked away.

Candelaria took the path to her son's house, stepping into a freer state of mind, feeling a sense of relief, as though released from her worries. Familiar with the pathway through the tall oat grass, she wondered how many times she walked its narrow course to go to the blacksmith shop and livery stable. She might bring her husband his lunch or tell their children it was time to come home and do their homework. Sometimes, it was to ride their horses. This time, however, something felt wrong to her and, momentarily disoriented, she stopped. A large owl screeched, swooping overhead, having flown out of the barn. They liked to nest and roost in the rafters, she recalled, suddenly remembering her vision of a man walking with a grass stem in his hand. On this path, she realized... He came to her son's funeral. The man who brought Sylvia Sumner! Tucker Stewart. Candelaria instinctively recognized the vision was a premonition about her son's death.

Avoiding the house, no longer wanting to see it, she chose a side pathway into the pines, enveloping her with its hushed and calming stillness. She came out onto the driveway, crossing it to continue down another familiar path through the trees, the one linking this house to her mother's. Bending low under the pine boughs, the grass still green, she continued following the path more by memory than by sight. It was becoming lost, overgrown and unused. The familiar approach to her parent's house was no more. She expected to see a burned structure, but there was none. Over a year passed, nearly two, since the fire. While eeriness and suffering pervaded the area surrounding Jim's old house, here the clearing was empty and silent. Only the peaceful forest remained, as though there had never been a house in this place, and the experiences of those who once lived here never occurred, nearly seventy years of history erased. In the grass and weeds, she stepped onto the concrete walkway once leading to the house, then the two low steps, and nothing, for nothing was left, only a small forest clearing.

Candelaria felt the night caress her aching and worried body and mind, like a softening, a tender sighing through the fir and pine. She closed her eyes and it was there, the house and its families, all their stories yet alive. Her grandma, Lucy Shoseegan, was a native woman who married her Papa Berto Mendoza. Shortly before he died, he stood by the garden with her grandmother. Her eyes were closed and her face turned upward to heed a call to reverence. This is what Candelaria now did, seeing her grandmother with her hat, like an upside-down basket, woven of plant fibers and decorated with beads. It was her Mama Stefa who lived with them, having never married, and only having the one child, her mother, Ev Garcia. Now, though, it was Grandma Lucy she felt holding her, loving her, soothing and healing her.

"Oh, Grandmother." Candelaria expressed her love in tender whispers. "I never got to know you, not really, but I am here now, feeling you and loving you, too." She put her arms out and raised them up toward the stars barely visible through the tree tops.

"Thank you," she said to all her grandmothers she could now hear singing in the air surrounding her. Effortlessly, it came to her. The wind lightly drifted through the trees and, like waking from a dream, the experience passed. She opened her eyes and turned to go home.

CHAPTER TWENTY-SIX

Ev knew the little girl her family nicknamed, Ellie. The last time Ev saw her, she was but a toddler with sticky fingers and food smeared on her face. She loved candy and ran around her brother-in-law's house wearing only a diaper that needed changing and a tiny shirt. Her black hair was drawn into a ponytail so short, it stuck straight up in the air. One day, a grown woman in her twenties showed up at Ev's house, needing a place to live. It was Aurelia Mendoza, Ellie. She had become a stranger.

Ev welcomed her. Keeping house and feeding herself became a full-time task once she got old. She needed someone to help. The young woman had a car, too, a necessity for an elderly woman, living at the furthest end of Pine Way as she did, nearly two miles from Edenville. She liked the girl, but her affection did not extend to Ellie's boyfriend. He worked on a forest service fire crew at a nearby station. They responded to more than one fire near her house. That fact raised suspicions in Ev's mind. She asked Ellie, a nickname for which she never cared, "Why does that boy always show up where there's a fire?"

Toying with Ev, Ellie gave a smart-alecky answer. "Because, he's a fireman?"

Ev insinuated that he was a fire *bug*. She informed the girl he was no longer welcome at her house. Whether Ev saw something or had a feeling, she kept it to herself. She advised Ellie not to have anything to do with him and, then, her house burned down.

For months afterward, Ellie's boyfriend reminded her, "That old lady's dead because of you." Her misconstrued adulthood fell away on the day she finally reported him. Frightened, with no place else to go, she stepped onto Candelaria's porch, tucking an envelope under her doormat. When the door opened, she retrieved the envelope and stood.

The unexpected visit from her mother's housekeeper terrified Candelaria. An incident with her sister came to mind. Gilda was impatiently combing her hair, the tangles catching in her comb. Trying to force it, she got madder, yanking at her hair until the comb snapped. Only then, did Gilda cry, her cancer diagnosis revealed earlier that day. Aurelia Mendoza's presence frightened Candelaria, for she was yet grieving that loss, pain buried beneath the accumulation of other, more recent losses. She hated Death for the life it wrenched from her. She hated it as though it were a thief who stole what was most precious to her, what she valued most of all.

It was a difficult moment, a personal one. Nevertheless, she welcomed Ellie into her house, as though in surrender, quietly offering to her to sit at the table. Once seated, the young woman slid a faded yellow envelope across the worn wood tabletop, where stains and burn marks ceased to matter. Candelaria opened it and read the letter it contained, full of Ellie's emotional outpourings of remorse and regret.

Setting the letter on the table, she asked, "Why do we do this to ourselves?" Letting that go, she told Ellie, "You did nothing wrong. You have nothing to feel guilty about." To further reassure her cousin, she said, "You reported him, and that was the right thing to do. He destroyed a lot of property." Drawing a handkerchief out of her apron pocket, she wiped her eyes and blew her nose.

Ellie started to cry, easing the burden of fear and guilt from her weary, young shoulders.

Candelaria got up from the table and wrapped her arms around the young woman. "You're fine," she said. "You'll be just fine." Hugging her affectionately, she acknowledged, "We both will. We'll both do just fine."

Grabbing a paper napkin for Ellie, she changed the topic. "So, I don't get how we're related. I don't remember anyone mentioning you, or ever seeing you before you came to live with my mother." At the kitchen counter, she poured them some coffee, but Ellie said, "No, thank you." Returning to sit at the table, she tucked one foot under her and propped her elbows on the table, holding her cup with both hands, slowly sipping, waiting for Ellie's answer. She wore slacks now, finding them more comfortable.

Ellie always wore pants, blue jeans, and tennis shoes. This time, she wore a short-sleeved, blue, red, and white plaid blouse, tucked in, with a leather belt. Her short, black hair was smooth and shiny, worn in a pony tail, though no longer sticking straight up, and her bangs parted slightly.

Answering Candelaria's question, she said, "My grandfather, Manuel Mendoza, was your dad's brother."

Candelaria, at first surprised, grew serious, trying to place the information. "My Uncle Herman never got married... Oh, my Uncle Manny!" She was baffled. "Why didn't I know that?"

Ellie shrugged her shoulders. "I knew your parents. They'd come to visit us."

Aurelia Mendoza was much younger than Candelaria's daughter, yet she spoke of things that required her to search through old, childhood memories for a clue. Unable yet to place the girl, she further questioned, "Where did you live?"

"With Nana Shoseegan's family, at Laketon." Ellie pointed her head in that direction, adding, "Up in the mountains, by the lake."

Candelaria only visited her father's family when she was a girl. She remembered very little of their visits. After her father died, she never heard of them again. Incredible loneliness suddenly washed over her, talking about these things. Her family was shrinking. To be confronted with the fact that there were relatives she never got to know, made her depressed, feeling cast off, like a boat that has lost its mooring. Yet, life is always changing, she thought, something new always coming in as something old fades away.

"Where do you live now?"

"Over at Hillview." Ellie again nodded her head to show Candelaria the direction. "In the apartments. But, I gotta get a job, cuz my boyfriend was paying the rent." Her gaze dropped to her lap, returning to her lost self. "I got evicted," she said quietly. Nothing else to say, nowhere to go, no job, no place to live, and having sold her car, Ellie hoped she still had family. Thankfully, Candelaria invited Ellie to live with her, for as long as she wanted, adding the enthusiastic wish to reconnect with relatives in Laketon. Speechless, Ellie was relieved to hear Candelaria's kind offer, but she figured no one was left in Laketon to whom either of them could claim a connection. She appealed to Candelaria, because there was literally no one else to whom she could turn, except Candelaria's brothers and their families. Ellie was not about to approach two old men for help, she thought. Candelaria, her second cousin, was her last chance. Her self-confidence and self-respect fell to their absolute lowest.

Candelaria sincerely believed that, if someone could have prevented her son's death, lifting him out of his darkness, he would still be alive. Helping Ellie was a chance to give someone what she wished had been given her son, a hand up, a friend in need, someone who cared who could have turned him around. Why all those who strived to help him had failed in the endeavor, she wondered, was a question left unanswered. Trying to find the reason, only brought her more pain, so she eventually chose to let it go.

• • •

Tragically, there was one person who knew how much Candelaria's son had suffered. Jim's wife, Beth, witnessed the harm he was capable of inflicting upon himself, each time she bandaged another cut, each time she drove him to the infirmary for stitches, and each time she held him close to her as he cried.

"I'm no good," he said to her. "I should be dead!"

Beth told him through her tears, "Stop saying that, Jim! You're a good person!" She held him in her arms and rocked him, like one would a small child. Where they sat on the kitchen floor, spatters of blood marked the scene of Jim's latest self-inflicted horror.

Their home lay in shambles, not because they cared less about it, but because they had no energy, lacking the ability to pull themselves out of the low places in life. Jim established his self-harming habits long before he and Beth married. Yet, she married him anyway. Though others may have seen glimpses into Jim's secret, she was the one who lived with it. Likewise, he was the only person who knew about her past, what her mother's boyfriends did to her before she ran away from home. While they may have married what others call, "damaged goods," they stood by one another for sixteen years. It was more than they could tolerate. The day Jim Hart died was the day Beth Hart left him, neither of them able to tolerate it anymore.

CHAPTER TWENTY-SEVEN

People assembled in the elementary school auditorium for the first Edenville Historical Society program. Years passed since Jim Hart's death. His sister, Rosa, became a teacher at the school and founded the historical society, along with several other community members, like Tucker Stewart. Cleaning up the old newspaper office one day, he found a myriad of old photographs. One of them was a color-tinted, turn-of-the-century picture of a large house beside the blacksmith shop and livery stable. He had the picture mounted on heavy paper and placed it on a painter's easel for the program. This very large photograph included an eight-year-old Walter Henry, his father, Henry Henry, and Jim and Rosa's grandfather, Tim Hart, who was a young man at the time. They were standing in front of the barn, posing for the picture.

Walter Henry stood beside the photograph, telling everyone about its history. "Now, this here's a picture of Pine Way's oldest business. It was built by my father, Henry Henry. He and my mother, Henrietta Peabody, were among the first settlers to this

valley and built the large house you see next to the barn there."
He pointed at the picture. "It was torn down a long time ago."

Candelaria, among those in attendance, remembered her
mother saying she was raised in the big house that used to be next
to the barn, and that *her* mother was the housekeeper. She had
no idea the old ruin from her childhood days was the same
building as the beautiful country inn featured in the picture. She
paid close attention to his story, not wanting to miss anything as
the old man continued to speak.

"It was a wayfarer's station, like a hotel. The blacksmith shop
and livery stable were like today's gas station. There was a gold
rush in these mountains here, and people came from everywhere,
including my grandpa." He slipped his hands into the back
pockets of his overalls. "He married my grandma after that gold
rush petered out and they settled in the big valley and raised a
family. He always talked about making a way station for people
to stop at on their way to and from these mountains.

"Around the time of the Civil War, lots of people were
comin' out West here and needed stopping places to rest and take
care of things. Well, my dad got married and he and my mom
decided to build that way station. Eventually, people who were
passing through ended up staying, and a little town grew."
Pausing, he looked over at everyone, seeing them enraptured and
quiet, before he continued, "You know, this whole area used to
be known as Pine Valley, because it was full of trees, all forest
here, where the town and all the houses are now. Little by little,
the trees were cut down by the settlers. They used the wood to
build things, like their homes and outbuildings. Then, they
planted fruit and nut trees, like the ones you see all over this
valley. After awhile, there was only one area left where there was
still some forest."

He hesitated momentarily, stopping to drink some water from the glass Rosa handed him. "Anyway, people started to picnic in that last grove of trees." He looked away from everyone before abruptly concluding, "And that's about when it happened." Stopping altogether, he drifted back to his seat.

The audience murmured amongst themselves, looking at one another, until Rosa said, "Thank you, Walter, and everyone, for coming."

The audience wanted to know what he meant. Someone stood up and asked, "What happened?"

Rosa addressed the old man. "Walter? Would you like to answer that?"

He began mumbling something about having talked long enough and it was unimportant, but Rosa encouraged him to continue. So, he stood up, sauntered over to the front of the audience, and reluctantly began to finish his story. "Well, about that time, I was just a kid and used to help out around the station, feed the horses and whatnot. This one day, I was—" and he stopped again.

Rosa placed her arm around him to reassure him. "It's okay, Walter. You don't have to tell any more if you don't want to." She felt sorry for him, looking so weary.

Tucker, however, wanted to hear the rest of Walter Henry's story, so he planned to meet him at the barn the following day.

Walter Henry still went to the old blacksmith shop and livery stable even though it was no longer in business. The people who owned the feed store in Edenville, rented the building to keep supplies, hay, and feed for their store in town. The old man mostly sat in the sun. Sometimes he raked or carried out small chores around the place. Occasionally, he talked about the old days to whoever happened by and cared to listen. He was there the next morning, a Saturday, when Tucker arrived with Freckles, the German Shepherd that used to belong to Sylvia Sumner.

Camera around his neck, Tucker started taking pictures right away. When the two feed store employees left to deliver some hay, he took the opportunity to grab a stool and sit in the sun next to Walter Henry. Thinking he might continue his story, Tucker was pleased when the old man brought up the subject.

"I couldn't tell the rest of my story last night with Rosa and her mother there, and all of Rosa's kids."

"Oh?" Tucker reminded himself not to sound too eager, but wanted to encourage his storyteller. "Why's that?"

"It was about when Rosa's great-granddad killed my dad," Walter Henry answered plainly, yet with a tinge of sadness.

Shocked, Tucker stared, nearly breathless. He heard the story long ago, but he believed it was legend, not fact.

Walter Henry began telling the rest of the story, pointing here and there as he spoke, which helped him to dramatize what took place nearly eighty years ago, in the 1800's. "It was right out here a-ways, right in front of these buildings, where it happened. I was just a kid back then, came out to see why my dad hadn't come into the barn yet."

He interrupted himself, wagging his finger at Tucker. "Now, you got to promise me, you won't tell any of this to Rosa and her family." He forgot he heard the story shared more than once amongst the family.

Tucker agreed. "If that's your wish, I won't tell anybody."

Satisfied, Walter Henry resumed. "I came out to look for him and he was over down the road there, in front of where our house used to be. He was comin' down this-a-way, along with an old Indian fella, Hector Shoseegan. Josiah Hart was there, talkin' to them. That was Rosa's great-granddad. They were arguin' about somethin'.

"You know, back then, people would carry a gun in a holster." He smiled a bit. "It was the real, Old West here, at one time, Indians and everything. But, old Josiah pulled out his gun and shot my dad dead, right there before my very eyes. Before I knew it, Hector shot *him* dead. Hector was my dad's friend...had a son named, Dexter...gave Little Jimmy a dog." He quieted down. He had no teeth, or nearly so, and sat there working his gums, dripping spittle out the corners of his mouth, his sagging eyes watering.

Tucker wondered, "When did all that happen, Walt? Do you remember?"

"Oh, you're asking the wrong person," he answered. "I can't even remember the year I was born." He laughed lightly and slapped his knee. "You get old enough one day and you'll find out how all the years start to run together." Trying to suppress a grin, he pointedly warned Tucker, "You'll see."

Enjoying his story, Walter Henry lowered his voice as if someone might overhear the next part. "But, you know," he said, "I think old Josiah Hart was really an outlaw."

Having fun, Tucker likewise lowered his voice and asked, "No kidding?"

Keeping his voice low, the old man said, "Oh, yeah, he wore them guns, a double-holster, mind you. Not everyone wore those." He picked up a stick off the ground and began using it to draw in the dirt from where he sat and, when needed, it became a pointer stick. Raising his voice, he corrected himself, "Except Hector, then his son, Dexter Shows-His-Guns. Everybody called him that, cuz he wore them guns, I think even after it was against the law to wear them." He chuckled a bit, looking far off, talking quietly, "Yeah, old Dexter, practically the last of his tribe." Pointing with his stick, he said, "That family used to live near the old picnic grounds over that-a-way, oh, way back. They were still living in them bark houses. Saw one once."

They were quiet for a bit. Walter Henry scratched himself here and there, squinting like he was trying to remember something. "So, after that gold rush died down and the Civil War ended, and them pioneers kept comin' out West here...there were a lot of men, loners, shifty-eyed and hungry, with nothing to do, no one to answer to, except themselves. The country was all in a state with that new construction." He glanced slyly at Tucker.

"Oh, you mean *Re*construction?"

Walter Henry grinned. "Yeah, that, too," and laughed with Tucker.

Freckles stood up, stretched, and wandered into the barn to get out of the sun for a while. She was still familiar with her birthplace and, while the stalls were gone, there was plenty of straw upon which to lay. Tucker kept an eye on her. Once she lay down again, he almost asked another question, but Walter Henry picked up the story.

"He showed up here, Josiah Hart did, wearing them guns, just his horse, a rifle in the scabbard, a bedroll and...had on an old, threadbare Confederate uniform." The very idea of it disgusted Walter Henry. "Pssh! He didn't fight in no war. That was before I was born. But, my dad never trusted the man, even after Josiah married his sister and settled down and built a cabin, had a family, and everything." Walter Henry stopped talking again, as though this was all he was going to say.

Tucker wanted to hear more. The Hart and Henry families went way back, but he had no idea how close they were to each other, related through this terrible man, Josiah Hart. He felt as though he had stepped into the past, with the old blacksmith and even the decrepit barn as his guide.

"Anyway," Walter Henry spoke up suddenly, as if he had been asleep and woke up, back into his storytelling. "Josiah Hart wanted to name this whole area here, Pine Way, ready to fight over it, too. My dad said he settled the place, it was his choice, and he wanted it to be called, "The Way," or some such name. Oh, boy, that riled old Josiah. 'The Way?!' He says, 'Over my dead body,' and my dad said he'd like to accommodate him, yelling at him, 'Ever since you came here, Josiah Hart, wearing those *fan*cy guns, you've been trying to take charge like you were a king or the pres-i-dent, him*self*!' My dad was worked up." Walter Henry laughed and cried at the same time, for the story of his father's murder was also a tale of two stubborn men. Neither wanted the other to be right or to win the fight. "Well," he said, pretty much all talked out, though wanting to finish his story, "once they got onto the subject of presidents and even slavery, that did it. Somebody was gonna come out dead and it was my dad, right over there by that last elm tree." He was quiet for a few minutes, then Johnny arrived to take him home, so they said their goodbyes.

Standing alone outside the barn, Tucker got an idea. Since no one was around, he impulsively decided to climb up to the hay loft. Feeling ridiculous and, at the same time, disappointed, he started climbing down again, when something caught his eye. It was as small as a nail head, like a purple or lavender pearl. He reached across to the board it was stuck to and pulled it out, turning out to be an earring, its post having been pressed into the wood. He recognized it and slipped it into his shirt pocket. Calling Freckles, and not getting her attention, he coaxed her out the doorway.

Locking the door, Tucker grew concerned that Pine Way's blacksmith shop and livery stable was becoming only a story told to schoolchildren, like the great forest that once filled their valley. The barn's fate had tolled, it seemed, and it was succumbing fast, slowly receding into the dusty background of life. In his imagination, he could almost discern the ragged storyteller, withdrawing into the forest to be reclaimed, no longer needed. The image left him with an ominous feeling.

CHAPTER TWENTY-EIGHT

Tucker opened the door to what had been his grandfather's, then his father's newspaper office. Ascending the stairs, he found it remarkable he had climbed them nearly every day since he was a child. Each individual step in the stairwell he committed to memory for their particular creaks, splinters, and stains. Grab the handrail here, but not there, his father's voice carrying up the stairs, "Watch that one step, Tucker James!" He forgot and, with the loud crackle of the wood, came his father's anger, "I thought I told you to watch it!"

"Why are you so hard on the boy, T.H.?" It was Herman Mendoza, sticking up for him.

"Boy's got to learn to be careful," his father said.

His mother showed up with lunch and a quick kiss for them both, never able to make the trip up the narrow stairwell. Too hard for her, she said. "Too *fat*," he heard his father say. Tucker waited all morning for that lunch, because he made it himself, without his mother's watchful eye, for she was distracted with news of the war weighing heavily upon her mind.

"Tucker James? What are you up to?"

"Making our lunches!" Now, he had to make his father's lunch, too, to undo the lie he told her.

"Mind, you, go light on the—"

"I know! I know!"

"I couldn't get to the market, either, so . . ."

Everything she forbade him to use and everything she reminded him to conserve, he laid on thick, and packed his lunch. His mother stepped into the kitchen. He heard her behind him, knowing exactly what she looked like, hands on hips, with that expression on her face that said, "What am I going to do with you? Hmm?"

He stopped what he was doing, but she said, "Never mind. You scoot. Your father's waiting for you. I'll be along with your lunches after I go to the market."

Crestfallen, his special lunch in danger of being rationed, like the rest of their lives, he trudged toward the door, but not without his mother holding him back with a firm, yet gentle hand on his shoulder. She unexpectedly pulled him toward her, hugging him from behind. She held him so close he could hear her girdle shifting under her dress, so close he could feel her steel-belted bra on his shoulders as she rocked him side to side, humming a tune, like a lullaby.

She sniffed and said, "I'll never get to hold your brothers, ever again," referring to the dreaded letters that arrived, each time one of his older brothers was killed at war.

"Get along now," and she patted his behind to hurry him along, a little more hopeful, yet a whole lot more guilty.

This particular visit to the newspaper office became more like that day in 1945, the year his mother, Addie Stewart, died. Within the musty interior, fear and uncertainty now loomed, like the old, black-and-white movies of the war, when bombers flew overhead and children huddled in the dark, sheltered places below.

Moving on, for he had other things on his mind, he entered the upper story of the newspaper office, fully prepared to admit he came for something other than work. It was shut down, and had been ever since Jim Hart's death, thereabouts. Cleaning the place was not on his mind, nor investigating its history. Today, he entered as a spy, deftly tuning out the memory of his mother's voice and ignoring the stray newspapers and loose scraps, the pencils, pens, and paper clips strewn across the floor. Spiderwebs swayed in the light wind of his passing, like a ghost, approaching the front window, daring to revisit one evening, several years ago.

To his inward-gazing eye, there came a scene now gone into the past, yet still able to bring an aching fear to his heart, Sylvia dashing across the road below the office, the puddles rippling from the chill wind, and everything yet wet and green from recent rains. He drew away and turned his attention toward the rear window. Fulfilling his suspicions, an old pathway, still visible in patches, led behind the brick buildings, from the road to the back of the barn.

Withdrawing the rescued earring from his pocket, he held it to the light streaming through the window—for understanding? Reasons, perhaps? Slipping it into his shirt pocket, it occurred to him he felt sorry for Sylvia. Ever since they were children, when she turned to his family for love and protection, and to be with those who cared about her, Tucker pitied her.

Although, he could not deny that he loved her, too, and still felt the need—

"Why would she want to marry me?" he beseeched the walls around him. "After what my dad did to her mother? After Jim Hart and—" His voice broke into tears and he knew, above all,

"She didn't need another husband." Without further hesitation, he went down the stairs and out the door, swiftly locking it as though to flee that ghost he had become.

It was not enough. He had to go around to the back of the buildings, where Sylvia— Desperately fighting with himself, because he wanted to stop what he was doing, he followed through with it, because he felt compelled. Turning to walk down the alleyway, between the newspaper office and the old general store, he prepared to retrace her steps that one Easter Sunday in 1967. For some reason, he paused to look back toward the rear of the barn. In his oft-dreaded remembrance, it came to him, Jim Hart standing by the sink outside, waiting for Sylvia. Jim's patience was soon rewarded. Tucker knew this for a fact, because a co-worker witnessed their entire meeting from the upstairs rear window of the newspaper office. Tucker dismissed the man's lurid play-by-play comments at the time. Thinking of it now, incredible pain stirred within his heart, a heavy, unbearable pain. Why he remembered this next piece, he was at a loss to explain, but it would not wait for his approval.

They were in high school. Jim quickly pitched in to help Tucker's father unload the paper on which to print that evening's edition. The delivery arrived late, so they were scrambling, his father in a hurry. In their rush, Tucker caught a glance at Jim's arms, the scars from self-inflicted gashes, like a meshwork of scar tissue. Jim wore long sleeve shirts with the sleeves rolled down, but this one time, Tucker saw. Jim unrolled his sleeves, glaring angrily at Tucker, who was scrambling to pretend he saw nothing, as though distracted by his father's sudden ire. "Now, mind about that ink, son!" Once a grotesque sight, Jim's scars now affected Tucker differently, as something heartbreaking and tragic.

Stepping through the alleyway, Tucker's search continued, out to the road and to the path beyond. Yet, the way to Jim Hart's house only existed in the past, for he was met with a wall of overgrown bushes and weeds. Only then, was he released from his determined effort to face the truth, and to escape it.

He looked for Freckles and discovered she was chasing after rabbits. "Freckles! Get over here!" She ignored him, he believed, taking off into the bushes after every slight movement. He soon learned there was no cause for worry. The German Shepherd curtailed the chase and ran to him, panting, then tiredly walked alongside until they arrived at home.

Seating himself on his front steps, Tucker held the obscure piece of jewelry between his fingertips, examining the tiny artifact for the story even it had to tell. One earring can destroy an entire house, he thought, for it belonged to more than the insignificant pair he bought his mother for her birthday one year. They were not cheap, originally, though from the thrift shop, they cost him a whole thirty-five cents. "Pearl Drops," he recalled the name in silver script within the black, fake-fur-lined gift box they adorned. Shimmering with a grape-lavender, pearl-like luminescence, they daintily dangled from a single post, set in silver, the kind of earrings its wearer would need to have pierced ears. She never wore them, because his father confiscated them, saying, "Your mother doesn't have pierced ears, son." Evidently, Sylvia had worn them. Tucker never knew about the little gifts his father gave Sylvia's mother, but now he imagined the ill-gotten line of descent. Whatever had been Addie's, became Charity's, and then Sylvia's, like a pair of earrings never meant for her ears.

He walked out to the road and tossed the earring as far as something so minuscule could possibly be thrown, off into the field, back into the past where he very much wanted it all to be, by this point. At last he felt reassured, finally ready to relinquish a very painful dream. Now, the truth could be seen.

"She was just a friend."

The only witnesses to this final affirmation of truth were the old elm trees lining the road, planted by the hands of all their forefathers. They dared to stop at a random place along the endless road from here to there and call it Home. Because of their decision, Pine Way and Edenville became his home.

He wanted to hear more of Walter Henry's story, all he knew, which only these elm trees were left to share, the sole survivors of a long and continuing history. Inside his house, he gathered his journal and pen and returned outside to sit on his porch. Opening his journal, he began to write, "The story never really ends. It is like a beautiful stream in one's imaginings, the story of this place where we live. Its surface shines on its restless trek 'cross the valley where one may dip and follow it for a-ways, whether upstream or down, and never finish it, nor know of its source, for even there, the spring upwells from out of the earth, itself. The fountainhead, I firmly believe, is that place from out of which all good stories arise, flowing upward and outward, to one day catch the wind and carry on. In this place of origins, you see, lives the story of old Pine Way."

CHAPTER TWENTY-NINE

A sudden rain shower began to pour outside Ev's home. Her husband snored quietly, having fallen asleep while reading the newspaper. She peeked through the living room window to her garden, then toward the overgrown lawn, watching her grandchildren dashing across it. They were caught in the rain shower on their way to her house. Ev noticed Rosalita had outgrown her dress. She was becoming tall and skinny, while Little Jimmy had not grown past his baby fat stage. He was only five, going on six, and Rosalita was nearly nine years of age, running with her schoolbook over her head to keep her hair dry. They made it to the porch as the rain passed and the sun began to shine. She could hear them, their child voices. They were out of breath. Curly was shaking out his wet fur.

"Don't let the dog in the house," she instructed them.

They used a towel by the back door, inside the porch, to dry off. Little Jimmy impulsively decided to stay outside and play with Curly, so Rosalita said, "Okay." They threw a stick for the dog, or a ball, whatever was lying around.

Ev's husband got up from his chair to go into the kitchen and pour himself another small glass of the cheap wine, of which he already drank two glasses. Ev told him to wait for dinner.

"I'm not cooking for a drunk," she said, half teasing him, half serious.

He held the bottle in one hand, his empty glass in the other, and replied, "Who are you calling a drunk, *mujer?* I will drink my vino when and how much I please," and began to pour. Raising the glass to his wife, he gave his final word in the matter, "Salud." A car drove up to their house, so he set the bottle and glass down on the kitchen table as Ev followed him out to greet their visitor.

"Who is it?" Ev inquired, trying to see over her husband's back.

"Wait a minute!" Like two fussing old chickens in the chicken yard, Ev's husband, Jesse, was irritated with her. "Back up! I can't open the door if you're in the way here!"

"I'm not in the way," Ev argued. "You're just too drunk to do anything! Let me!"

"No! No!"

The door popped open as their visitor, Dexter Shows-His-Guns, came up the walkway to their front porch, his grinning face revealing missing teeth, with Ev and her husband grinning in return.

"Uncle Dexter!"

Dexter greeted them. His faded jeans were held up so high by suspenders, the waist was nearly to his chest, exposing his white socks on his sandaled feet, the toes separated where the sandal thongs divided them. His undersized flannel shirt was unbuttoned at the cuffs, but he was happy, even without his guns.

"Come on in, Uncle Dexter," Ev welcomed him. The children joined them. Soon, their house filled with boisterous activity.

Dexter's long, braided hair was entirely gray, while his eyebrows were jet black, which Ev noticed and found humorous. He and her husband went into the kitchen to sit and visit. Curly was dried off, but he was made to stay on the porch, because his damp fur smelled like sweaty, dirty socks. She began cooking dinner for everyone, simple fare, some tortillas, some meat and chiles, and leftover pozole.

After a while, Dexter discreetly set a small pouch on the table. "Hey, Jesse. Got something I wanna show you."

They talked quietly between themselves. Rosalita and Little Jimmy began to fidget.

"Can we have cookies, Grandma?"

Their grandma had baked peanut butter cookies for them, but she told them to wait. "No, no. Here, have some meat. Here, in a tortilla." She handed each one a meat-filled tortilla, the meat hot and greasy from the sizzling pan. The dog jumped on them, barking, whining, and begging, until Little Jimmy dropped half of his filling.

"Jimmy!" Rosalita accused him, "You did that on purpose!"

She knew he wanted cookies right away, but their mother and father showed up before either could get any. So, Ev quickly filled a sack to give them.

Dexter set his great-grandnephew on his lap and hugged him. "Hey! How's my boy, eh, Jimmy?"

Needing to leave, the children hastened to greet their parents, while the two men remained in the kitchen, drinking wine and talking about the old days. Ev missed seeing the small gun Dexter bought for her husband as a gift, a derringer, made to be concealed in a pocket or a purse. She followed the children outside to kiss them goodbye and to talk briefly with Candelaria and Big Jimmy.

"Hello, you two!"

Cheerful and smiling, she held her arms folded in front of her. Her apron was stained from cooking. Her housedress, basically worn every day, and her slippers, were wearing thin. The bright-blue scarf on her head lost its newness years ago and had become faded and frayed.

They watched the children play with the dog on the lawn, getting soaked, with the sun shining brightly on the pine and fir trees, still dripping from the rain. Everyone was laughing.

That singular moment in time, that tranquil scene in 1940, Ev Mendoza relived twenty-five years later while flames consumed her house. Encapsulating a period of her past when the children contentedly played, it represented a fulfilling stage in her life when the whole family looked to her for a place called Home.

Years of memories swiftly burned, her own childhood beginnings in Pine Way, living at the way station with her mother, the same playing and running while her mother worked, then living with Jesse. She once thought he was so handsome. They tended their garden and their own fruit orchard. Her husband's family visited. Her mother lived with them. Laughing, eating, and telling stories filled their lives. She cooked for everyone, while Candelaria and her sister and brothers played and ran into the woods. They loved to follow Ev's mother on one of her quiet forays into nature, always with a walking stick she found.

"Ay, Mamá." Ev's heart grieved for her mother, the roof falling in and ashes blowing up, the thick black smoke dwindling as the firemen sprayed it with water. "I miss you, mi mamá, mi pobre mamacita," referring to her mother's nightmares and her awful, debilitating fear of fire, having never recovered from seeing her parents burned alive in their prairie home.

When Ellie tugged on her arm and everyone grew impatient with her, wanting to leave on the march to the state capital, Ev wanted to drop down to the ground and die, for her life was done. The house, her home for the past sixty-five years, ever since she was only twenty-five, the place of all her joyful memories, her happy home, was dying before her. She knew she could not go on any longer.

Whispering, "goodbye," to the house, to her dreams, to her children, her grandchildren, she let go, turning away from the life she loved, to instead walk toward her death. The people she walked with that day, to her, had become her guides-come-a-calling, having assembled to bear her away and take her home. She went willingly, knowing her time had come, at last.

EPILOGUE

Walking along Pine Way Junction one evening, the night's mystery full and pressing inward, Candelaria breathed it in, nurturing her wounded heart. The dusk came upon a sighing breath of wind, blowing through the tall grasses, softly rustling their dried stems. The crickets began singing all at once and the lights from each house began to shine. The bark of a dog, a door banging shut, and a woman's voice, yelling to her children, were but dissonant sounds somewhere else, somewhere so far away they could not reach her. It was as if she were in love again, in love with the deep mystery, in love with life.

Taking a shortcut through the alleyway she had known since her youth, secretly meeting her husband, Jimmy Hart, before they married, she remembered the excitement, laughing with him, being loved by him. She was a teenager when they met and he was in his twenties. When they were seen together at the Pine Way picnics, oh, how the other women bore their envious eyes into her young and innocent gaze toward them. He loved her as much as a man can love a woman, and he yearned for her, being made to wait for the wedding, after she turned eighteen years of age to his twenty-six. He waited and, today, Candelaria felt glad they did not succumb to their mutual yearnings and visit that same loft her son would, years later, take Sylvia Sumner.

When Candelaria returned home, she lingered on the porch of her house, where she hoped to one day no longer reside. Eventually, she went indoors, turned on the kitchen light, and sat at the table to write in her notebook about her walks in the woods. Picking up her pencil, she glanced around the kitchen. Noticing the warped, wooden cupboard doors and the drippy faucet, the bag of laundry by the door, she wrote, "Death has a way of settling old scores and wiping clean the slate listing our mistakes. Like a river washing over the land in spring, forgiveness comes and cleanses the heart."

She recalled Jim placing a box under the house. Taking the flashlight she kept by the door, she went back outside, around to the spot where she thought he might have placed it. Beneath the little, weather-worn shack where they were stored, sat the cot and the chairs from her mother's viewing, tucked away neatly. Everything under the house, as she shone the light around, was stored very precisely. She spotted a crumpled, old cardboard box, and froze. She dared not touch it, for it was not her's. It belonged to her son and to her mother. Waving a hand through the air, she dismissed her reasoning. "Oh! It's mine now," she said. Carrying the box, she smelled the strong, acrid odor of smoke lingering upon the items it contained.

For a short while, she sat on the front steps to watch the last light fade from the sky, until all that remained were stars-a-million, swept across the night sky like scattered fragments of light-dust. "Good night, Mamá," she whispered to her mother. "Good night, Jimmy. Take care of our son." Her heart swelled with love, the pain from loss still fresh, so deeply the wound was dealt. She yearned for an answer to her question. "He was a good boy, wasn't he?" Tears filling her eyes in the quiet intimacy of her soulful intercession, the answer came to her and filled her with its truth. On this day, this night, she swept aside all falsehoods, without question, all that she ever wrongly believed about her son, and asserted proudly, "He was a good man!"

THE END

THE END

NOTE FROM THE AUTHOR

Word-of-mouth is crucial for any author to succeed. If you enjoyed *Mothers of Pine Way*, please leave a review online—anywhere you are able. Even if it's just a sentence or two. It would make all the difference and would be very much appreciated.

Thanks!
Corrine

ABOUT THE AUTHOR

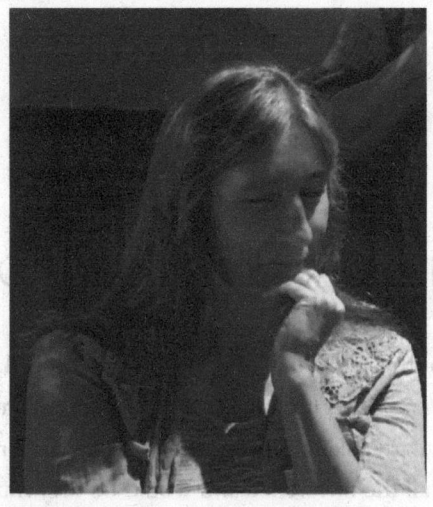

Corrine Ardoin grew up in a small town and has lived in many rural locations around California. She enjoys writing stories and poems, gardening, and hiking the trails near her home. Her dream of getting published came true when she received a grant to write *A Natural History of the Nipomo Mesa Region*. Her first novel, *Fathers of Edenville*, established her career as an author. She currently lives in California with her husband, Dan.

Thank you so much for reading *Mothers of Pine Way*.

If you enjoyed our book, please check out
Book One of the *Pine Valley* series!

Fathers of Edenville by Corrine Ardoin

"If you love a good story written with loving detail,
Fathers of Edenville is for you."
–Matthew J. Pallamary, author of *Land Without Evil*

www.ingramcontent.com/pod-product-compliance
Lightning Source LLC
Chambersburg PA
CBHW011134100726
47898CB00009B/2975